DEVIOUS
PILGRIMS

DEVIOUS PILGRIMS

A Novel

Ron Savage

NEW PULP PRESS

Published by New Pulp Press, LLC, 926 Truman Avenue, Key West, Florida 33040, USA.

For information contact:
Publisher@NewPulpPress.com

ISBN-13: 978-0692718995 (New Pulp Press)
ISBN-10: 0692718990

Printed in the United States of America
Visit us on the web at www.newpulppress.com

To dearest Janny

DEVIOUS PILGRIMS

How can I regret my life
when I find the blue-green traffic light
on the corner delightful against the red brick
of my house. It is when the signal turns red
that I lose interest. At night
I am content to watch the blue-green
come on again against the dark
and I do not torture myself
with my shortcomings.

- David Ignatow, *The Signal*

Prologue

THOUGHTS DURING THE LAST VIEW

City Morgue, Calle Vasquez
Palencia, Spain
May 3rd, Present

THIS IS MORE a look than a viewing – an identification, Name The Body. She thinks of it as a one question quiz show with no prizes.

Lili (*Leelee*) Mack sits on a rusted, fold-out metal chair in a small room that has mint green cinder block walls and a smooth gray concrete floor. Soon the coroner will roll out the gurney – or whatever the shit they do, all she has to go on are TV shows.

God, my tits are freezing. Her hands and shoulders feel cold, too. Her shoulders keep quivering. First she thought her shakes were nerves, the whole Hanging Out With The Dead business, now she's thinking maybe it's the room's temperature. If Lili had known this place would be so frigid, she'd have brought kindling and a Bic.

Her skinny legs are crossed at the knee, lovely legs but not as lovely as they were in her twenties and thirties. In her twenties and thirties men wrote bad poetry when they saw those legs. She's wearing a faded chocolate colored t-shirt with the words Snake River Rafting written in cursive across a modest breast line. Her denim shorts are mid-thigh length and freshly washed so she can look halfway

1

presentable. But the man who has now become The Body had always been a piece of *dreck*. It wasn't like she owed him a Bergdorf ensemble.

"Buenos dias, senorita," the guy says, rolling in the gurney. He's maybe ten years older than Lili, fifties easy. He introduces himself as Dr. Padua – tall, lots of combed back dark brown hair, much of it graying, a decent looking man. Then he says, "Es usted un pariente?"

"I don't speak—" she stops; tells him, "—No lo entiendo."

"—A relation, senorita, are you the wife, the sister? A re*lat*ion."

She waves a back and forth no-no. "I'm just here to identify, that's all."

"—Good enough."

Lili has been doing what she guesses people do in this sort of situation. Going over past events – the last month or so – trying to sort it out. She is thinking about how every eyebrow twitch gets bronzed and becomes "history." And you can't talk your way out of history. There is no history hustle. If it happened it happened. History isn't like, say, Justice. Justice has a blindfold and scales. It'll listen to your arguments. It can be seduced by your sincerity, your logic.

You can get justice to go your way.

"Would like to view the deceased privately?" Dr. Padua says.

"Yes, please." And as an after thought, "—Nothing personal."

He gives her a smile that's minimal. "They'll dress him, you know," Dr. Padua says as he's leaving. "—Fix the wounds. Comb his hair, that sort of thing."

They could give his evil ass a fire ride, I won't be offended, Lili thinks. Who cares how this creep looks. Comb his hair, really? Forget his hair. You can't make it up, these guys want him to look attractively dead.

Yes, history is different than justice.

History doesn't play well with others. It won't chat with you or listen to reason. Arguments will always get ignored. History is a family album and whatever you did goes into that album and stays in that album and nobody can sneak it open and tear out. Your page.

Shit is what shit is.

Lili Mack folds down the sheet across The Body's chest and looks at its face.

"Hello, asshole," she whispers, touching its cheek with her index finger. How many people touch the face of the dead? How many know the dead are gray and rubbery and cold?

"God, you look terrible," she says.

There are four bullet holes in The Body's head. One in the right temple, two in his cheek, and one above the right eye.

She notices the left eye's open slightly. The smell isn't that great, either.

Shooting this hideous bastard dead was the most satisfying act she's ever done in her forty-two year life on planet earth – better than sex or feeding the poor.

Lili once heard how the guy who dresses the dead Superglues the eyes shut. *Don't want the ole eyes popping open and giving little Auntie What the Fuck a coronary.* Lili half expects the thing on the gurney to read her thoughts and give a smirk.

But nothing.

All right. Fine.

People need to make sure the dead are truly dead and not waiting for everybody to get comfortable. That's what Lili believes, no Zombie rising with outstretched arms and saying, "Hey, sweetheart, only kidding," and taking a chunk of your face.

"—You done, senorita?" Dr. Padua has opened the door halfway, checking on her. "Is that our man?"

Lili Mack covers the face with the sheet. "He's not as good-looking as he used to be, but it's him."

"Are you all right?"

"I started feeling angry all over again."

"The dead deserve our respect, senorita."

"Good people deserve respect," Lili says. "Sorry, Dr. Padua. What can I tell you? This particular jerk deserves a tub of Piranha."

She has her father to thank for what happened – *his* plan, *his* wish to step over the line, the self-absorbed Raymond Mack's idea of realigning the world. "America's Artist," people called him that. It's how he liked thinking of himself. But what would those people say now? "It will be a scare he won't forget," her father had said; told her to let him take care of it. "Don't you think the man deserves a scare? He ruined your life, for godsake. Oh don't look so worried – it'll be nothing extreme, nothing fatal. Scout's honor, sweetheart."

Raymond Mack had lied.

FUN AT THE HOTEL DE PEREGRINO

Pamplona, Spain
April 12th, A month ago

SHE'D WALKED OVER to *his* table. *We need to get the Who-What of this from the beginning.* Dr. Grigor Bolian is pondering recent events, separating the scheme from fate. This one definitely falling in the fate category. He'd been sitting outside the hotel café at a two-seater table, sipping a glass of white and people watching.

Alone.

That's the important word, *alone*, nobody bothering anybody. Grigor didn't ask for this; he didn't plot or plan. No traps were set, so-to-speak.

Jessie Cole introduced herself with a little quiver and a half full whiskey already in her hand. An intelligent person would know the details of this woman before feeling her damp palm, seeing the jitter in her shoulders. The doctor had inhaled her scent. He could smell the pheromones.

Lets create a personals ad, shall we? Grigor thinks.

Mid-fifties, looks totally early forties. Curvy lady 38-32-43, 5'3", 132 lbs. A sun and fun sort of gal. Can adapt to many lifestyles. Your happiness is number uno! Just divorced but not letting that get me down.

Forty minutes later they are in his hotel room and naked.

"Oh c'mon, darling, tighter." Jessie says this when he ties her wrists with the silk scarves she'd given him — yellow, royal blue, cherry red. "Don't be a pussy," she says, an attempt at humor, then she does a snort-laugh.

Now the doctor wants to poison the bitch just for that stupid laugh. Mushroom tea is the best way. Mushrooms can take six days to a half-month to kill a person, mostly kidney failure. More than enough time for him to travel elsewhere.

"—Maybe too tight," Jessie says. Her fingers have gone numb.

"Just keepin' it real."

"You're *so* ethnic."

Amanita Ocreata. Ramaria formosa. On occasion Dr. Grigor Bolian will whisper

the names to himself. Isn't it poetic, almost symphonic? Listen. *Gyromitra esculenta.*

Boletus subvelutipes. Amanita phalloides. His passions live in shadowed ground, under spruce and pine, amid Douglas-fir and oak, the beech trees and eastern hemlock, laurel and rhododendron. Many gather in fairy rings.

Fairy rings, can you believe it? Such a kick.

"I'm not a tea person," the woman tied to the headboard says. Her thighs and stomach are fleshy, pale and loose, a Jackson Pollack spray of blue veins. "Tea gives me gas. Believe me, darling, that's not an ordeal you want to go through. Talk to my ex, I'm sure he'd have stories to tell."

God, really? Grigor can't believe it. *Pity the dear boy.*

Some mushrooms have a white, cottony veil, some come with pores of scarlet and brilliant orange, others pale yellow, others a bruised, inky black. Dr. Bolian will discuss these creatures to anyone who shows the barest interest. He will spice his narrative by describing how efficient each kills.

Recently he acquired a new employer – an artist whose work he's always admired, particularly the man's bullfight sketches.

One wonders if they have fairy rings in Spain.

"See what you do to me?" Jessie says, "See how comfortable I feel? I can even discuss my bowels with you."

"I'm honored." A forced half smile.

This afternoon Dr. Bolian brought one of his favorite mushrooms to the hotel, the *Amanita ocreata*, a.k.a., the Death Angel. When discovered and picked, it has the look of a small, circumcised penis.

"Perhaps you could order me another whiskey." The woman nods to the empty glass tumbler on the floor by the bed. "Bourbon beats the hell out of tea."

"Oh you'll love this tea." He doesn't want to think about the woman flatulating. Bad enough he has to see her naked. An hour or so ago he'd taken off his clothes. Just before that, Bolian had placed a folded square of paper, something like a tiny envelope, next to a coffee cup on the nightstand. Now Grigor taps the powdery contents into the cup. "It's an aphrodisiac, you know."

"*—Good, very good,*" comes a whisper, not from the woman but from a place inside Grigor Bolian's brain. *"Go for the potions, that's the spirit!"*

Today the disembodied voice Grigor has named The Commander is doing its very best to guide his life again.

"Oh and let me give you additional kudos!" The Commander says. *Congrats on being practically invisible. Best look for a man in your circumstance, my friend.*

Average looking men are perfect for all sorts of clandestine ventures. But you must work on your walk. Too cocky. Too I'm Letting You Live in My World, if you my drift. One needs to develop a humble walk." The Commander has a Reaganesque quality. Oh, it's unmistakable. He is Grigor's invisible boogeyman, his Hollywood Ah-Shucks cowboy.

"—Are you listening to me?" Jessie Cole going all pouty on him.

"You are in my every thought."

"I'm being serious here."

The commander is right. Dr. Bolian does have other business, more important business. The artist, Raymond Mack, has sent the doctor two sets of photographs, three of his daughter, Lili, and three of Isaac Stalin, his target, the man he's been hired to kill. He only needs to see the photos once but he is a man who likes to cross his "t"s and dot his "i"s. He keeps the pictures in the inside pocket of his tan linen suit coat.

"Is 'Bolian' an American name?" The Commander again.

"It's Armenian," Grigor says, the umpteenth time. You'd think the bitch would pay attention.

"Your men grow fine mustaches."

"No one in my family wears a mustache."

"—Excellent. Eighty-three percent of the men in America don't wear facial hair, either. It says, 'I must hide my face from you. I am a man with secrets' No facial hair, no secrets. This is bullshit, of course, but it sounds right to people, sounds honest and American."

These thoughts are interrupted by the woman.

"Did you tell me the tea was an aphrodisiac?" She's perked up.

"That's what people say."

"—What people?"

"Orgasms can go on for hours."

"—What people?"

"Those in the know."

"Is that the truth?" Flirting with him; actually batting her eyes. "Are you sure you don't want to take advantage of little me?"

The woman is totally naked and tied to the bed. Dr.

Amazing has fucked her twice. Advantage taken. Points scored. It's the tied up part that excites him. Grigor wonders what parallel world the female creature calls home.

A breeze goes through the open windows of the hotel room, billowing the gauzy white curtains, the air damp and chilled. The northwest part of Spain has showers and clouds in April.

"This should be great fun," The Commander says. Grigor pictures his imaginary friend's head wobbling as he talks, Mr. Shaky Head. *"You're quite the card. Due to your Armenian heritage, no doubt. Are the Armenians similar to the Jews? I got so tired of the Jews. They ruined my movie career, you know."*

Muted laughter occurs when Grigor ignores him.

He doesn't blame The Commander. Bolian is willing to accept his share of the responsibility. A man who kills for fun and money is going to get harassed by the paranoid movie-political types.

Dr. Grigor Bolian once diagnosed himself as a Schizophreniform Disorder in 1989, the year he received his MD at the University of Virginia, that winter roughly coinciding with Ronald Reagan giving George H. W. Bush the keys to the country. Grigor realizes his condition has lasted far more than six months, the limit for his original diagnoses. He should be calling himself schizophrenic by now, but he hates going there.

"Such a troubled expression, darling," the naked woman in the bed next to him says. The woman is a smoker who enjoys a good tan. Her bronze, dried skin has that cracked oil painting look. Her lipstick is faded from the day and the sex. The color bleeds along the tiny wrinkles of her lips. She tells him, "You are quite the lover."

"I'll order us a pot of hot water," he says. "It's tea time."

LONG BEFORE HER FATHER'S PLAN

City Morgue, Calle Vasquez
Palencia, Spain

LILI MACK IS still seated in her rusted foldout chair. The viewing room is empty now, the damp, sterile chill of the air conditioner blowing down on her. She's been trying to clear her mind of the awful images and smells, the mutilated head, the scent of him – of *it*, the dead "him," the once upon a time "him."

Lili knows when things started, exactly. After her father had ordered her to see the Puerto Rican social worker Margaret Ramirez. That's what Raymond Mack liked to call her: "The Puerto Rican Social Worker Margaret Ramirez" – like all of that was one name —no PC gene in that boy. Her father's new lawyer had found the woman. "Highly recommended," the lawyer told them.

"—Explore your feelings," Raymond said.

"I don't have feelings."

"Yeah you do, trust me."

"I *don't* need therapy."

How many years ago was that drama? She'd been thirteen then, so 1987. Lili and the old man had been together forever. Her mom died years ago, breast cancer at thirty-six. Marion Eva Mack was her name, friends and family calling her "Minnie."

Lili loved that name – Minnie. It was very close to the old Martha Reeves and the
Vandellas's song.

Minnie Mack, when are you coming back?
Never.

Her mom had been a nurse. Minnie Mack, RN. Her father, Raymond, said her mom was a gentle soul who had a lot of friends and acquaintances. Friends of friends, that sort of thing. People would call Minnie at all hours for comfort and the answers to medical questions. Minnie was also a religious person and liked to pray with her callers, either over the phone or in person. Many prayers had to do with medical matters but there were also prayers about family members who'd been acting peculiar or abusing illegal substances.

"You remember your mom, honey?" Raymond had wanted to know.

"—I dunno, a little."

"She adored her girl, you know."

What can a person say?

Lili doesn't remember much about her mom, perhaps Minnie coming into her bedroom late at night after an evening shift and kissing her cheek, maybe the smell of her sweat and vague perfume. Most of Lili's nurturing came from Raymond and various housekeepers employed over the years. But the truly Faithful Mother was her music, her cello – the mother who soothed her and wouldn't die.

Raymond gave the cello to his daughter for her fifth birthday; baby-sized, of course, and Lili took to it right away. There were weekly, private lessons, too, and nobody ever had to tell her to practice.

One of the housekeepers had nicknamed her, "Little Miss Perfect" because of Lili's dedication, her total focus.

How else does a person learn?

Lili didn't care what people called her. Well, okay, she *did* care. But she cared more about learning the cello than what others *thought* about her learning the cello.

Her practice time didn't vary, three to five – the time

she came home from school until time for dinner. Lili practiced the way the post office delivered mail, *"Neither snow nor rain nor heat nor gloom of night,"* etcetera, etcetera, would stop her from putting that bow to that string.

Period.

"I don't want you pushing yourself too hard," her father had told her, over and over, really, different times in different words but always with worry in his voice. This time she was ten, maybe twelve. "You're a kid, you know – have fun, be with friends.

Have a sleepover, go to a movie, whatever you guys do."

"What's wrong with wanting to learn something?" Lili said, not that she didn't love him for being concerned about her. This day was a winter afternoon, ice nestled in the corners of her bedroom windows, the place where she practiced. Then Lili said, "People who do this *have* to do this, don't they? Music ... or drawing pictures. Weren't you like me with your drawings? I bet you drew stuff all the time."

Her father didn't answer. He just kissed her forehead. Maybe that was his answer. He had his I Pity You look.

Lili remembered that afternoon and that look.

Years later she understood what that look meant. She'd been playing in a string quartet at the Germantown High School library when the thought had occurred to her, such a delayed revelation – in her early or mid-thirties. *You don't get to choose, do you?*

It's not, 'I think I'll get an MBA and sell Whole Foods.' What were they playing that night? Lili couldn't recall. Bach, maybe. But she'd stopped counting and missed her cue. *No, this shit will choose you,* she had thought, meaning any type of art – music, painting, tap dancing, it didn't matter. *Art is a compulsion, not a choice. It's dope.*

Devious Pilgrims

You long for the feel of the needle, how the body loses it's spine and it's tension. Or maybe for you it's the smell of the weed and the way it fills the lungs and the peace that it brings.

Music definitely did that. Her favorite Puerto Rican Social Worker Margaret Ramirez told her that years ago.

LILI'S THERAPY

Glenside, Pennsylvania
February 18th, 1987

"CAN YOU HEAR me?" the therapist says, a Puerto
Rican accent.

"You sound far away."

"But you *do* hear me?"

"—Not as good as I'd like," the girl says. She's thirteen
years old, a skinny, quiet thing with thready dark hair and
skin white enough for a cave dweller. Then the girl says,
"It's better than last month, of course. Last month I
couldn't hear shit."

Margaret Ramirez likes counseling teens. Their moods
go through them the way tornados go though the Midwest,
shifting, cataclysmic. She's been a clinical social worker for
thirteen of her thirty-eight years, mostly with young
people in the Philadelphia suburbs.

This is her first session with Lili Mack.

"So that's an improvement, yes?" Margaret believes
thinking positive will right the world but she has also read
the otolaryngologist report and knows Lili hasn't been
nearly outraged enough.

"I'll never get my full hearing back," the girl says.
Margaret notices the words are without emotion. Lili
could've been saying pass the salt, or that greasy burger
joint down the road is out of fries.

The social worker and her client sit across from each
other in padded corduroy chairs. The office is on the
second floor of a four story building overlooking a park
that has a gray dirt path and wood benches. Sunlight goes

through the branches of tall trees. Shadows quiver on the green and brown floral wallpaper.

"Hearing is very mysterious," Margaret says. "You could very well get the entire hundred percent back. Believe me, I've seen cases like yours. It could happen." The voo-doo of bad thoughts isn't allowed.

"I *know* I won't get my full hearing back," the girl says.

The otolaryngologist's report describes Lili being pushed into a half–filled pool of filthy water during a Christmas party by the boy giving the party. Logs were in the water to keep everything from freezing. The boy who was having the party then locked the patio door and refused to let her back into the house.

Imagine: soaked to the bone, 11:40 at night, 37 degrees. More than that, a mix of rain and snow – Margaret has no trouble imagining any of it. Oh she knows clients have a way of letting their therapists feel the feelings they themselves can't manage. But that's okay with Margaret. The dirty pool water and the cold left Lili Mack with an inner ear infection that stole her hearing, but the infection became exacerbated by a mycin drug, a double whammy, the boy and her doctor conspiring, each in their own way.

"Your Dr. Greenwald is very optimistic." Margaret forces a cheery tone. The "optimistic" part is true. The report does say Lili will get her hearing back, just not a hundred percent.

"Greenwald is a dick." Lili says, mostly to herself.

"Granted, okay." The therapist, giving her that. The guy sounded like a dick on the phone.

Margaret's fingers are interlocked, hands resting on her protruding stomach. She wears a burnt orange and aquamarine tent dress, a Hawaiian muumuu, the sort that's loose enough to hide a person's fat. She's sure it doesn't hide anything. People know you've got a nightmare body if you wear this stuff. But what can a person do?

Hey, be proud of your body, Margaret thinks. She has spent more than one night alone and naked with a bottle of chardonnay – studying the thick flesh that camouflages her wished-for figure. She has even screamed at the mirror.

Lili is talking about her music. Margaret knows about the girl's music. She had gone to a school recital to hear her nephew play piano and heard the girl play, too. Angels couldn't do a better job. Who could be so skilled and still be a child? There is something unnatural about it – no, "stunning" is the word. The social worker has talked to the father, too.

His majesty, Raymond Mack, an ego waiting for a national holiday.

"America's artist," that's how far a few souls have gone. *More hype than ability,* is her thought. Margaret reads the *Times,* the reviews. She takes the occasional trip to the big New York galleries. Yet in the social worker's more chardonnay drenched moments, she spars with the man. Raymond Mack has always seen his daughter as no more than an appendage, another glory feather in his heavy-handed glory hat.

His daughter's failure is a disturbing shadow on his life, a mark of imperfection.

This has less to do with Lili's lost of hearing than the fickle wheel of justice not turning the way our divine Christian God intended.

"—You aren't allowed to look at your hands when you play the cello," the girl is saying. She watches the pine wood floor as she talks. Her voice is always on the rim of being heard. The sentence is a non sequitur. The way a boy will ask a girl on a date when she's in the middle of talking about being grounded for two weeks. Lili wants to discuss the cello. Her future in music, if she's got one.

"How old were you?"

She looks up at Mrs. Ramirez. "When I started? Five. I had a little chair and a little cello, and I scratched my way into music. That's my dad says, 'You scratched your way into music, Tootsie.' I can't believe I said that." Lili rolls her eyes and giggles but keeps looking at the pine floor. That's what daddy called me – 'Tootsie.' You know, like a nickname or whatever."

Margaret is thinking about the music part. "I like that," she says. "—What you said, 'Scratched your way into music.' I can see the little girl in you doing just that."

"Most times, I feel like her."

"What's the number one worry?" Margaret already knows the answer.

"I can't hear the notes like I used to," Lili says. "—And I'm supposed to have a competition next week, a scholarship to the Casaux in Madrid. Me and a person from my school are competing."

"Is the person a friend?"

"He's the guy who pushed me in the pool."

AMBIVALENCE ABOUT STALIN

St. Jean Pied de Port
April 12th, Present

RIGHT AWAY THEY'D have to walk up a mountain and down again, from St. Jean de Port to Roncesvalles, that's the *first* day. 24 kilometers, close to 8 hours. April is a chilly, rainy month, too. Maybe he'd get an infection of his own.

The mountain air can give a person ideas.

Hey, don't wish that on anyone, Lili Mack thinks; does a little shiver. Then she reconsiders. *Since when don't you believe in symmetry?*

An eye for an eye.

An ear for an ear.

Lili is sitting outside on a red plastic chair under an awning at the café Eden. The small tables are plastic too but a chartreuse color – eternal Christmas in the Pyrenees. St. Jean Pied de Port is a beauty with its narrow streets and canals and tiny bridges, its two story white stucco homes and salmon colored shutters. Lili is waiting on her new love. *Can forty-somethings still say that – a new love?* She doesn't understand how it takes a guy an hour to wash his face. Whoever heard of being late for a pre-hike drinky? But that's him – the too clever Mr. Isaac Stalin. Yes, the same name as the Russian, and, yes, similarities went beyond the name.

Now Lili describes her companion to the waiter and wants to know if Isaac's wandering about looking for her.

"He's not arrived yet, madam." The waiter's English isn't half bad, better than Lili's French. He is an older man – her father's age, maybe – white hair combed back, someone who manages seedy and elegant simultaneously. He says, "I will be on the look out."

"How 'bout some *fromage* and some bread, *s'il vous plait.*"

"Any particular *fromage.*"

"You be the judge."

"Madam honors me."

"The guy looks much younger," Lili says, not wanting the waiter to miss Isaac. "Mid to late thirties, like that. Receding auburn hair. Exceptionally long fingers, you know, almost porcelain-looking – very beautiful fingers, a musician. Not what you'd call faggy – not that there's anything wrong with that – but you get what I mean. You can't miss him."

"Quite handsome, I'm sure."

"He's all right." *Let's not get carried away.*

Now the waiter is saying, "Would madam like more wine?"

She looks at her empty glass. "God I'm a sucker for wine."

"Shall I take that as a 'yes'?"

Lili nods, pushing her glass toward him. The waiter bows and pours the wine in one move. This somehow amazes Lili and she mutters, "Well done."

Neither she nor Isaac are spring chickens. Lili is forty-two, Isaac four years older. He has never been married. "The cello is a demanding mistress," he actually says to her, a little too often and a little too seriously.

Like why wouldn't I understand?

Lili Mack tells her new friend in one of their nightly phone conversations that she'd married an "overly attentive person." She says, "We were very young, our early twenties., late teens, I forget. I didn't know how to handle his kindness. I mean I found the guy near his car on the side of the road – the middle of nowhere. *Lansdale*, for godsake. So I call 911, what any person would do. Some driver sideswiped him and left the scene, knocked him into a ditch. Anyway, the marriage lasted a month under six years."

"That's a long time nowadays," Isaac says.

"—I guess, I dunno."

"How was he, what sort of man?"

"—Extraordinarily intelligent," she says. "I'll give him that. Norman Pearlman, was his name – *very* self-absorbed. I mean, you can't imagine." Lili wanted to know if her new soul mate had ever heard of him. Isaac didn't think so. "He became famous, you know, writing books and all." Lili recalls her joke about them, "Norman is the only astrophysicist who believed the universe revolved around me. Ha, ha."

Silence.

Really? Once in awhile Lili didn't get Isaac Stalin. *That's a damn good joke, you bastard. How bout a polite 'pretty clever.' Something?*

"... so yeah, okay," Lili says. "I'm still flattered, though. I'm not perfect, sue me. All I can say is, it's true, be careful what you wish for."

Norman gave her everything she wanted, whatever he could afford; and in those early days, what he could afford wasn't very much. "I wouldn't be here if it wasn't for you, Lili girl."

One of his many gifts was a T-R 3032 Maga-d hearing aid. The best at that time, a $3,200.00 piece of high tech which he bought at 175.00 a month for the rest of his life, or so it felt at the time.

Then she'd been neither deaf nor dumb. Yes, her hearing had lost it's fine tuning; and, yes, she did complain to Norman how 4ᵗʰ position on the "A" string drove her crazy and how these little things had cost her professionally.

"You do the best with what you have," Lili would eventually say.

Thank you, Norm. You're killing me with kindness. And I'm going screwy with all your gifts and good deeds, but I get it, I really do.

Thank you.

Lili Mack looked down at her glass of red. She looked about the Café Eden and the tourists walking the gray cobble street of St. Jean Pied de Port with its shops and outdoor market stalls.

A mental note to herself: *don't treat Isaac Stalin the way you treated Norman.* Everybody goes into a relationship with baggage, that was her thinking now. Middle aged people just start with deeper suitcases.

Wait, wait. I keep thinking this is for real. What a dope I am. This isn't the start of a "real" relationship. She couldn't keep all that straight, what her father wanted and what she mostly wanted, not that she'd rule a real relationship out. You can't just dismiss a person. *Wait, never think that. This is the start of something, but it's definitely not a 'give your heart away' thing. It's the start of our symmetry.*

—*Yes, very excellent ... symmetry.*

A person doesn't have to do much to find the wrong sort of anything. Go down this path rather than another. Lili likes thinking about the ins and outs of fate. Curiosity can do more than kill cats. Yet what would life be if we didn't take a chance or two, bend our comfort zone? If we play it too safe, pleasures are lost. She's come to realize that, too. Plans and maps will help us if the world isn't misbehaving, but how often does that happen?

They met again online at Pair-Up, a dating service who

advertises,

Tired of bad dates and being alone? Our scientific matching technique will find the life mate for you!

Lili saw Isaac Stalin on the Pair-Up website and she'd shown his photo to her father, Raymond, who agreed – that was the boy turned middle-aged. That was the boy who'd pushed her into the pool then locked her out of his house on Christmas eve, the boy who did that and another thing she hated thinking about – *a despicable thing, but let us not obsess, not now.* There is also a scar above her right eye from her fall into the pool. Three stitches, what an ugly mess it was, though the years have made her scar close to invisible. The boy let her walk home, too. Lili shakes her head as she thinks about it, a mile and a half, her clothes and hair drenched, wind blowing a mix of snow and the rain about her.

Lili decided to go with Pair-Up.

She'd ignored the Isaac Stalin part of her past for too long.

"You've let him getaway with robbery," her father tells her, tells her more than once. "You should've won that competition. Studied in Madrid – that's one school you can't buy your way into. You were always better than that prissy little shit. You need to grow a pair, sweetheart."

"Girls don't do that, daddy."

"I want to know you can do what needs doing."

Last June Raymond Mack – a painter known for his excesses – found out he had prostate cancer. The doctor reassured Raymond that he would die of old age before his prostate took him, but the painter had a sense of the dramatic and wasn't the sort who'd let an opportunity pass. He knew how to play the Make-Your-Life-Right-Before-I-Die card with his daughter. The more her father talked revenge – "righting what's right," was how he put it – the more Lili felt the old anger and resentment toward

Isaac Stalin.

"I have a good life," she would say, two-stepping away from it.

"You could've had a *better* life."

"I feel blessed, daddy."

"Gratitude will steal your fight," he'd say.

Lili hated their talks. Hated remembering how much she wanted to hurt Isaac. She didn't like thinking about hurting people.

"That's not me, she'd say to her father. "I'm not that sort of person."

"Everybody's that sort of person."

Nobody argued with Raymond Mack. He knew how to shut you down and keep you down. Lili wanted to tell her father how only the people involved with the situation – whatever that situation was – knew what was better or worse for them, but Raymond would have said that was a lie. He'd have said, "People like to hide those pieces of themselves."

She couldn't disagree with that.

Pair-Up gave its clients psychological tests. Only after the Idaho Personality Inventory, the Minnesota Multiphasic Questionnaire and the Welt Depression Scale did girl finally meet boy. She likes the idea of fate and science bringing them together.

She likes not purposely choosing him.

Maybe they wouldn't be compatible. Tests are not infallible. Maybe science would let her escape the expectations of her father.

To be safe, Lili chose to call herself Delores Reo. The years had passed, yes, and Isaac had never been a "pay attention" sort of guy. Why reveal herself until she had to? Her father thinks Delores Reo sounds like a forties movie star but he lets it pass. His daughter has a point.

Why let a decent revenge fail because of transparency?

She has misgivings about retribution – hates any form of extremism – particularly the sort of plan her father has in mind.

Raymond suggests hiring an assassin.

"I'd pay for it, of course. You'd never know."

"—But I know *now*."

Pair-Up had listed Isaac Stalin as one of six compatible choices.

TEA TIME AT THE HOTEL DE PEREGRINO

THE PHYSICIAN MUST pretend he is not himself. *I will be a kind man, a good listener.* These are the qualities the woman tells him she needs in a partner. That's how she describes the lover she will never have — "a kind *partner*, a partner who gets me, what I'm about. You know, equals."

Pathetic, really.

The woman wants to keep her wrists tied to the brass railings of the headboard with the scarves. Grigor Bolian is feeding her the mushroom tea a sip at a time.

"It's so *earthy*," the woman says.

"—A very special mixture."

"Aren't you having any?"

"Ladies first." Dr. Bolian pats the woman lips with a linen napkin. "It'd be difficult to feed us both."

"You're such a thoughtful man."

He is deliberately slow, enjoying the moment. Too many rush their pleasures. A man should keep his lust in check. *I am a kind man, I am a good listener, and more than that. Watch me, my eyes, my smile, feel the way I touch you, listen to the gentleness in my voice.*

They're naked amid tossed and twisted sheets. The late afternoon has become a bronze-gold color, candlelight soft. The light goes through the open windows and across the wood floor and the white walls of their hotel room. The woman's skin is sweaty and wrinkled between her breasts, darkly freckled. This is what sunbathing and age will do. Even the golden light cannot hide her years. Red lipstick and black eyeliner are smeared and washed out from the sex.

Jessie Cole is her name, Jessie with the big phony tits. Bolian finds her disgusting. The doctor is amazed he had an erection. Perhaps her slow death arouses him, a death occurring over many days. Mushrooms are awesome. Erections aren't uncommon when he is killing someone. More than once he's had an orgasm.

"It's so kismet, doctor." Mrs. Cole actually called him "doctor" when they were fucking. Now she says, "I'm not sorry this happened, you know. My little clitoris is still humming. I'm vibrating all over."

Dr. Bolian can tell she wants him to say he loved it, too. He is a thoracic surgeon by trade but flirted with psychoanalysis in his rotations, even subjected himself to six annoying weeks of therapy. He is a man who *gets* the human condition, or whatever you want to call it. Grigor is sure he could've been a hell of an analyst. The tweed jackets, August abroad. So he understands the woman wants him to say he loved it, too. But he can't bring himself to do that – lying has its limits. He smiles now and kisses the side of her warm neck and whispers, "Give me a couple of minutes."

"Oh you're in*sati*able."

"It's my Armenian side, father's family."

"—Passionate people."

"My father's sentiments, exactly."

After feeding her the mushroom tea Grigor slips on his white boxers and walks over to one of the floor to ceiling windows overlooking a gray brick street where bulls run on July 7th, three months from now, give or take a day – the *encierro*, what drew the crowd at the *Festival San Fermin*. There are many bull runs in many countries but nothing compares to Pamplona. Grigor imagines the packed streets, the double wood fences that do no good, the twelve bulls with heads arched down and horns leading, the fleeing people who dare let themselves be chased. You have to be eighteen years and sober to let the bulls have a go at you. A bull can run thirty-five miles an hour and toss a person into the air like a couple of bones in a plastic bag. During a bullfight there is an on-the-premises surgeon who specializes in those type of wounds and there is a priest to do last rites. Both are on standby. In a Pamplona bull run, there's only luck and a good credit card.

"I'm getting lonely," Mrs. Cole says, all pouty.

"The male body can't be hurried."

"—*Very good*, The Commander whispers. He is always there, always the voice of encouragement and guidance. *These lovely, generous women must be educated to the ways of men. So mysterious to them. What can you do? They mean well like children mean well, and we love them for that.*"

"Maybe if you put in a good word." The woman gave two quick snorts.

God, I hate this bitch.

Bolian is forty-seven, a lean man of average height, a man who'd disappear in a crowd of two. This is a source of pride. He believes his charm is being a gentleman not remembered. Thinning dark hair and a narrow face, a fashionable hint of facial stubble, what's more ordinary than that? Nothing, absolutely *nada*, zero. It's Mr. America in the twenty-fucking-first century. It's the man in his office cubicle who doesn't care enough to personalize his area. No clever signs, no miniature library of two or three paperbacks to express his interests, no painted action figures, no family photos in nondescript frames, no lunch menus pinned to his patch of corkboard to reveal the likes and dislikes of his digestive system – *nothing, absolutely nada, zero.*

"I'm going to have to get my little pistol from my handbag," Mrs. Cole murmurs. It's a Christmas present from my ex-hubby Warren. He's a doctor too, you know."

"How would I know?"

"—Podiatry."

"—An honorable profession."

"Warren gave me the pistol so I could protect myself from men like you, that's what he said. It's a derringer, double barreled. Can you imagine? I mean why would I shoot a decent fuck?"

Put a lid on it. Jesus.

The woman is a diversion, something random, an event thrust upon him the way asteroids bump indiscriminately into each other. Dr. Bolian has business in Spain. The artist Raymond Mack hired him five days ago to kill the man who is dating Raymond's daughter, Lili. Grigor accepted the assignment without pause. Spain at the start of the bullfighting season will always be an offer better than any other. *"Let him know why you're killing him before you do it,"* Raymond Mack's only instruction. Grigor must tell his new target, a man named Stalin, *"This is for ruining the artistic potential of another human being."*

Fine. Money is money.

Dr. Grigor Bolian's first kill was his fat Uncle Revig, the dry cleaning king of Syracuse. Grigor was eighteen then, his uncle forty-three and fucking his mother every Thursday afternoon at the Holiday Inn. That would be Revig's brother's wife. Revig and Sako, Grigor's father, were two of a kind, argumentative, morally vacuous, scheming their way into the lives of the unsuspecting and needy, etcetera, etcetera, and they seldom got along. In fairness, the mother was a whore Sako met at a bar in Camden. None of it surprised Grigor. The boy should've killed the mother, too, but he was young and, let's face it, a person who kills their mother is a sick fuck.

If we could only relive our lives.

Grigor is now sitting on the edge of the double bed, testing the strength of the pale blue scarves tied about Mrs. Cole's wrists and the brass railings of the headboard.

"You never think of doctors as kinky," Mrs. Cole says.

"We've always been a secretive bunch."

"You would've liked me when I was young."

"I like you fine now."

"That's it, what a good student you are, Grigor. Such a quick learner, my prize pupil." The Commander's voice is thick with pride. Dr. Bolian feels this pride deep within his chest. It's a warmth, a calming feeling that lingers in the muscles and tendons of his being. To be praised by The Commander, what is worth more than that? *"This is the American man's message to our women. 'No, my dear,' he says. 'No, I require nothing special from you. You are fine the way you are. American men will always be proud of their American women – we are charged with protecting and guiding them. And if not us, then who? This isn't simply American, it's Christian. Handed down by God almighty, praise His name. American men are in tune with the Lord, Grigor. And it's our job to pass that word on right away. How else would our women know what is expected of them?"*

"—No you don't," Mrs. Cole is saying. Her voice is small, quiet. "You don't like me 'fine.' You think I'm foolish. An embarrassment. But I don't mind, I really don't. I'm grateful to you. It's awful to confess, but I am grateful." Then her expression changed from reflective to pained. She looked at him. "I-I feel all crampy. Sharp cramps ... here." Mrs. Cole looks down at her tummy area. If her hands had not been tied, she would've probably pointed to the pain. "You're the doctor, what'd you think?"

"It's nothing," Grigor says, and kisses her cheek. "I have that effect on women." "—Oh *you.*"

WHAT SORT OF LOVE IS THIS

HE IS A man of many obsessions – his music, his instrument, his clothing, his skimpy, departing hair – and especially his hands. Isaac Stalin is massaging lotion into his palms and long pale fingers, a twice a day régime. He sleeps in black silk gloves to keep the moisture from evaporating. Isaac has been known to play his cello in his silk gloves. He's sure the gloves protect the strings from perspiration.

Isaac has a strategy for all things.

Right now he's looking out the window of the crowded Infantil Santo Hostel that he and Delores Reo, his almost fiancées, stayed in last night. A hideous place and what he suspects will be the first of many hideous places. There are no private bathrooms, no clean sheets, no clean anything. These are not hygienic people. He doesn't shake their hands or stand too close to them. Pilgrims are a guilt-ridden bunch who'd gladly suffer bed bugs for Jesus.

Below Isaac is looking down at the gray cobblestone street. He's pressing the lotion into his palms and about his fingers while he watches Delores Reo sitting at the little café across the way, drinking her red and looking lost.

Not even noon and she's drinking. And getting all honest with himself, *Who am I kidding, right? We are soul mates, me and Delores. Sweet Delores with that amazing Lauren Bacall voice. Give me another two minutes and I'll match you drink for drink. This thing of ours is happening very fast.*

Last night he'd held her to him in the bunk bed,

moonlight all around them. Very beautiful, really. He'd looked at her face in the pale light, noticing a slight imperfection.

A scar above her right eye. An almost invisible scar. He'd shivered at the sight of it but did not know why.

Maybe a chill in the room, he thinks.

"This thing of ours" – like he's in the mafia. Like him and the crime bosses are on first names. They kiss each other's cheeks and pat each other's asses. They smile their Friend of Mine smile and ask about family and how they ought to get together real soon. His idea of the mafia is always germ free.

Isaac thinks about Delores Reo's drinking, again. Drinking isn't a game changer for him. It's a game enhancer. *Baby, your drinking is okee-dokee with the Isaac boy, believe me. Everybody hates drinking alone.*

But does he really love this woman?

Isaac Stalin thinks about that one, too. He isn't a guy who gets swept away by anything or anybody. He is forty-six and he's never been married. A dater, yes. A man of many dates – needs must be met, situations need to occur.

That's our animal nature, what no man can avoid, that's our affliction, but at some point a normal man marries, doesn't he? A normal man has a family, does the things normal men do.

Isaac has always played his life close to the vest until he met Delores Reo. Shit, now he doesn't know. He likes the sex, maybe loves the sex. She plays Enya CDs and dances naked for him while he masturbates.

For that, he takes his gloves off.

It's a new day for you, Isaac Boy. Hell, it's a new millennium. This is not what you do, is it? Letting other people block your way. Women will seduce you into taking your eye off the bouncing ball. Women are diversions best left alone. His wiser voice. His Don of

Voices. What doubts doesn't he want to share with himself? How about all of them. He'd like to shut his mind down. Give it a rest. *Where is the off switch to the What-the-Fuck-Are-You-Doing part?*

Delores Reo has dug into his brain. Delores Reo whispers to him at two or three in the morning and gets him all excited. Brought down by a titanium boner? Is this the same man who plays second seat cello at the Philadelphia Philharmonic?

Why, yes. Yes, it is.

He's still looking down at Delores at the Café Eden. At this moment, Isaac is grinning.

I mean look at you, Delores, who wouldn't be okay with it? You're like a movie star. Like an, I dunno, that skinny blonde in all those summer comic book movies. What normal guy wouldn't like that?

It's his Big Head-Little Head discussion.

Who can believe this life? Two months and here we are, talking marriage and doing demented stuff in France and Spain.

"Have a positive attitude, Mr. Gloom and Doom." She says this last Thursday during one of their two-thirty in the morning phone talks. Neither of them sleep well and their talks have become an avenue for getting through the night. "People call what we're going to do the *Camino de Santiago*, which is the name of our destination – Santiago. Or they call it, 'The way of the Pilgrim,' or 'The Way of St. James.' We can get to know each other."

"—What's to know?"

If you're a serial killer, for instance."

"Is that what you think?"

"I'm kidding, Isaac. *God.*"

The *Camino de Santiago* is a month long hike, a month and a couple days, really. It starts on the border of France and ends at the Cathedral of *Santiago de*

Compostela in northwestern Spain.

Delores explained the whole pilgrimage to Isaac.

"—And it *is* a pilgrimage," she says. "At the end of it, the church will give us a certificate that says all our sins are forgiven."

"I don't have sins."

"Everybody has sins, Isaac."

"—Not me, okay? I got nothing to hide."

"We're not talking 'hide,' sweetie."

"I'm an honorable man." He's thinking of the Mario Puzo book *The Godfather*. He is thinking how the Al Pacino character would discuss sin.

"I'm just saying, nobody gets through life without a sin or two." She sounded amused. Maybe she was thinking, what is it with middle-aged men and *The Godfather*? Isaac wasn't sure, really. Who could figure a woman's thinking. Why didn't they get the important things? Delores is saying, "—Understand? Just little sins. That's all, no big deal, no finger pointing or anything. You know, dumb little sins. Well maybe that's not true, not exactly. Some would say *any* sin is a big deal. But that's extreme – I mean, considering. I'd like to think of our vacation as a spiritual cleansing."

"So you actually get a certificate?"

"Oh absolutely, baby." Her voice is always hot on the phone. Isaac thinks she has that Let Me Suck Your Dick voice going for her, not that he'd want her germs on his penis. "They give you sort of a passport at the beginning of the trip," she tells him. "The pilgrim hostels sign it. You know, saying you've been there, slept in the land of bedbugs and all. That you're walking the walk, so-to-speak."

"Can't we stay in a decent hotel?"

"The way of the pilgrim isn't easy."

"It's pretty good for the hostels."

"Think of what it means to be free of your sins."

If Isaac is honest with himself, he does remember a sin or two. There was that girl – *what the hell was her name? Lee. Lee Something* – so long ago now. She'd been in competition with him for a position at the Casaux in Madrid. He had pushed her ass into the pool. *Lee what?* He couldn't remember shit, anymore. *Too bad she didn't break her neck, the bitch.*

He couldn't think of the name to save his soul.

Ha. Ha.

"Okay," Isaac says to his almost fiancée. "So if, for example, I wanted to murder somebody – I'm just saying – I ought to do it before we start the actual trip – *before* I get the certificate?"

"See, you do have a good sense of humor."

OLD MEN AND BULLFIGHTS

Madrid
April 12th, Present

THE PICADORS HAVE just dug their pikes behind the
hump of the bull and the wounds are close to the spine.
The men haven't done what they needed to do. They've
missed the flesh and muscle that could've let the wounds
work on the bull in a slow way, calming him, taking his
strength a little at a time. A tremor goes through the bull's
front quarters and across its big dark shoulders.

Picadors get paid one, maybe two hundred pesetas
each fight. They are not very bright men, so it's a wonder
they can aim at all.

Raymond Mack has a ringside, shaded seat in the
Plaza de Toros. He can see the animal shudder from there
– sweat-slick, wobbly legs. This is why the shaded seats
cost you. A person can see the bull sweating but you must
have many pesetas to both see the sweat and sit in the
shade and not sweat yourself. You must *be* somebody.
Raymond definitely has the pesetas and many of the
people in Madrid know his paintings and his career. Some
of them call him "Maestro" and "Padre." Of course, April
in Spain is a more cloudy than sunny month, but Raymond
likes to be prepared, even for sunlight.

He's been coming to Spain since his twenties to watch
the bullfights. He has never stayed, though, never set up a
home. This time Raymond rented an apartment in
Santiago to watch over his daughter and to make sure

justice caught up with the Stalin boy. Past crimes could not be ignored. That was Raymond's second thought after the doctor told him about his prostate. His first thought was a scenario on dying the bravest way possible. He wanted to face the most dangerous bull in Spain. He imagines raising the bull Semillero from his grave. More than that, he imagines flame and smoke coming from the nostrils of the beast. Raymond sees himself in this scenario wearing the Suit of Lights, an embroidered jacket of gold and blue sequins. Here he fights and succumbs to death in a way worthy of celebration.

The maestro has no fear! they'd shout. *See how he faces the bull! Such grace, such skill!*

Only after a satisfying death fantasy did daughter Lili come to mind. Certainly Raymond would not force his daughter to do anything she didn't want to do. No, he is a father who will give a suggestion, point out the issues involved, talk to her about the way of the matador. Did she know there were female bullfighters? The actress Bette Ford, the journalist Conchita Cintron, the artist Patricia McCormick, and the great Christina Sanchez and Marie Sara, these were all women of courage.

"You should follow their example," Raymond tells his daughter. He says this by phone the morning she left for Spain. "These women are heroes to emulate. Remember your mission. The past must be set right."

"I'll do my best, daddy." She doesn't sound forceful enough to him. Where was the fire, the wish to right a wrong?

Lili's mother was like this child – too dear for the world, not tough enough. A nurse, a helper. She got breast cancer in her mid-thirties and was dead within the year. *Just not a fighter*, he remembers thinking. His Minnie. And, yes, he did call her Minnie Mouse. Her blond hair would go white in the summer, a skinny thing with little girl tits. God, he loved her; missed her, too, missed her for years and years. He couldn't count the times he'd reach over to her side of the bed and touched the cold, empty space.

Just like her mother, no fight.

Raymond Mack is sixty-seven and he's as imposing as the quivering bull in front of him – his arms, his shoulders, his chest. He has white hair and a full beard. It's very easy to imagine Raymond getting drunk at a neighborhood bar and starting a fight with the man he thinks runs the show. No reason necessary. Did a good fight ever require a reason? He's the old buck who doesn't want to be mortal. On occasion he will tie his hair off in a ponytail and look like a cool old guy instead of a crazy old guy.

Raymond has been sketching the picadors and the bull. The sketches are done with a soft no. 3 pencil on a 8 ½ by 11 black spiral book. People in the shaded seats behind him attend more to his drawing than the bull in the ring below them. He has captured the anxiety of the picadors perfectly. How does a person do that, capture an emotion? The people who watch Raymond draw can't express that idea, the capturing of an emotion, but those who watch are watching him because he does that so well, better than anyone. Some have been to the Museo del Prado and know he is better than what's in the Museo. This is what Raymond Mack is thinking about their thinking. Raymond also thinks he could be way off base, but probably not. He has talked to too many of them who like what he draws not to know the truth.

The artist goes to Madrid every April to see the fights. When he was younger he also went to Pamplona in July to run the streets with the bulls. One of those summers a bull caught him and gored the back of his left thigh and tossed him into the crowd. That day everybody got out of

Raymond's way and let him fall onto the gray brick and crack a fucking rib. People actually applauded but it wasn't a bad thing. It wasn't *"Hooray for the man being gored and cracking a rib."* They were applauding the drama, man against beast – still, not a soul tried to catch his ass.

The Plaza de Toros de Las Ventas is Raymond Mack's favorite bullring. It is in Madrid's Guindalera quarter, the Salamanca district. Raymond would have paid a little extra for a shaded seat if people would accept his money but you don't take money from Raymond Mack – not the *padre*, not the *maestro*. He is what the magazine *Art Vision* called, in their sweeping fashion, the "eyes and brush of the American abroad."

Right now Raymond is waiting for the doctor, Grigor Bolian. *Armenians, who can trust an Armenian? They're no better than the fucking gypsies.* Raymond feels guilty thinking this. He pictures all the Armenians protesting some gallery or other displaying his work. Nobody holds a grudge like an Armenian. Raymond looks at his watch. Already Bolian is an hour late. Raymond has paid the asshole seventy-five thousand dollars to kill the Stalin boy – not that Lili knows. She knows something will happen, that Isaac the Prick, the once-boy-now-man, will pay for disrupting her dear and promising life. But his daughter isn't a woman who thinks in extremes. Raymond Mack is becoming annoyed. *You think the doctor would show up on time.* The tip of his soft, no. 3 pencil snaps with a twig-like sound and breaks away from the paper.

DRINKS AT EDEN

"**W**HERE DID YOU find this place?" Isaac Stalin wants to know, meaning the Eden Café with its red plastic chairs and chartreuse plastic tables.

"—In front of the hotel," she says, her dry sarcasm, taking a sip of the red. "You know, you walk out and *see* it."

"You're an amusing person." He sits down at the table, opposite her.

"Sorry. A little wine and I get unbearably funny."

Already they aren't getting along.

He waves away the apology and grins. "You're funny, okay? Who doesn't like funny?"

The day has started out very French, an off and on drizzle, a day aching for the tragic, the sweeping gesture, the stumble from grace, but in a sweet Isadora Duncan sort of way. Sophisticated. Carefree. Strangled by your own scarf.

Lili notices that Isaac is wearing black leather gloves instead of the beddy-bye silk ones. What he calls his "hiking" gloves. *Do people have hiking gloves? Is that a thing?* Lili guesses so. She knows zip about hiking. One foot in front of the other, what's to know? Like regular walking, only longer. The man who confesses to jerking off to the nightly sound of her voice also has a walking stick that is as tall as she is, five-five or so. Who knows what Margaret Ramirez might have said about that stick. Isaac is six-four and a little more meat on him than the stick.

We look like a couple of refugees, she thinks.

"Hickory wood," he says, noticing her looking at the stick.

"—Very dapper accessory."

43

He lays a gloved hand on her wrist. "You look great."

"—You, too." He did, actually. Look good. He wore tan leather shorts and knee socks. Lili half expected the man to yodel.

She remembers him on the phone a couple of months ago.

Isaac Stalin thought she was "a living doll," isn't that what he called her? As in, "Jesus, Lili, you're a living-fucking-doll, no kidding." Her favorite Isaac line was, "You got snake hips that won't quit." He says that when he's drunk, his words a little slurred. Isaac Stalin also said, "You look familiar – no, more like *feel* familiar. Maybe it's just your nature, or whatever."

She loved that part of him, that tilted attempt at self-analysis.

"I hope that's a good thing." The night he called to talk this shit was right after their first date – a couple of months ago – Lili was already in bed with the light out. The digital clock on her nightstand read 1:53 AM. She *loved* that he called, though. Loved the impromptu time of it, as if he had to hear her voice, as if he had his dick in one hand and the phone in the other. *Maybe "love" is too strong a word. "Really liked" would be better*, Lili thinks. This is followed by an internal scolding, *Keep in mind why you and Isaac are together*. Her father's totally right – when is he not – Lili must show herself she can do what needs doing.

Are you playing with yourself, Isaac? Stroking your Isaac's Willy? Please tell me yes. Isaac's little willy. Please tell me you called to jerk off to my voice. Nobody's ever jerked off to my voice, I don't think. Nobody whose confessed, anyway. "Oh, keep talking, bitch. God, God, do that Lauren Bacall fuck me shit." *It's such a great two in the morning, drunk sort of thing.*

"Have other people said that?" Isaac wants to know.

"—That you look familiar, I mean.

"Well not *every*body."

"—But some."

"A few, yeah."

"How many are we discussing?" He isn't giving up. "I don't mean, you know, boyfriends and all. This is not 'let's dig into Delores Reo's very private life,' I don't do that. Just a FYI, I'm not that sort of guy. Trust me, all right? I'm not a middle-aged, or almost middle-aged, adolescent. I *am* the sort of guy who *cares*, that's true, but I do it in a non-in-your-face way, if you get me. And let's face it, a lot of people don't – get me, I mean."

"Maybe you're not interested in being gotten."

"—Hey, exactly." A hesitation before he says, "...so how many?"

What the hell does a girl do with that? "I have one of those faces," Lili says.

Isaac Stalin doesn't remember her.

This is the funny thing, though she's counting on that – him not remembering.

Lili was fifteen the last time they had met. She'd turned forty-two six days ago. How many years is that – twenty-six ... more?

Isaac wouldn't have remembered her, anyway. A boy like him. A man like him. Now he's in love with her, but back in the day she had no name. She was a competitor without a name, that's how he'd seen her – the girl cellist, the one who might beat him and go to the Casaux in Madrid.

The thirteen year old with the legs. *You remember my legs, I bet. I saw you ogling them many times, like every chance you got.*

She and Isaac Stalin, how events and lives shift – he from Casaux and she with imperfect hearing, she imperfect enough for the Philadelphia philharmonic to reject her nine times.

*Un*believable.

Crushing. Depressing. In*fur*iating. Add your word here _____.

Lili feels – no, *knows* – she is the worst sort of joke, the sort of joke that keeps on giving, a perennial. Yes, she will admit to being off slightly, *minisculely*, nothing to get incensed over, nothing earth-shaking. Her C sharps aren't all that crisp, okay? Maybe her B and E flats have a problem, too.

What the hell, Lili Mack has her teaching job at Germantown High. She loves her students and her students love her back. Lili has taught high school kids for twenty-some years. One year she was voted "Most Favored Teacher." That's worth something, isn't it? She is what-you-call-it – *fulfilled*. Sort of.

Lili has a sip of the newly poured red. Isaac taps at his empty glass and she pours one for him. She and Isaac are the only two customers who sit beneath the green awning at the Eden Café. The light rain is turning the gray brick street dark.

"Maybe this isn't the greatest of ideas, this hike." Lili isn't sure of the whole pilgrimage thing. Then again she isn't sure of so many things.

"I'm definitely up for it," Isaac Stalin says. He beats on his chest twice with his fist. "I'm a man who accepts a challenge. I'm known for that. Once I say yes, that's it.

I'm committed. Ask anybody, I don't back down."

Isaac forces a grin and has another sip of the red.

This is going to be a long few weeks, Lili thinks. *How did I get involved in this shit? Love this guy? There are times I'm not even sure I LIKE this guy. Who likes somebody who purposely messes up your life?*

Incredible.

Lili could actually convince herself she didn't want the

life she'd give anything to have. That what Isaac Stalin did to her didn't matter. Lili thinks about her father and his whole post-pancreatic death tirade

    ... I dunno, we were kids, weren't we? Being cruel is what kids do best. God, daddy's going to hurt him. I know it, Isaac with his lotions and his stupid gloves. Is that what you call it – hurt? Isn't hurting the boy a nice word for killing him?

RAYMOND'S GIRLFRIEND

Santiago de Compostela
April 12ᵗʰ Present

HILLARY ANN TUCKER is known for her fine thighs. Hillary would say, "When you are thirty-two, everything you have is not eighteen fine but it's still fine enough." Raymond Mack brought her with him to Spain.

She and "Baby Ray" – her nickname for him – are living in an apartment less than a mile from the Catedral Santiago de Compostela, the end of what people call The Way of St. James. Baby Ray is sixty-seven going on sixty-eight and Hillary knows he's amazed that she adores him and has orgasms. Hill is shocked that great men could be so vulnerable.

"You're my life now," Raymond said to her. This was when they were strapped in for the flight from Philly to the Santiago de Compostela. He was gripping her hand, readying himself for the take off. "If we die in the fucking ocean, we die together."

"Hey I'm not *that* committed."

"What are you saying?"

"—Dying-in-the-Ocean committed." She recalls glancing nervously out the planc's little window at the runway. "I'm being honest, okay?"

"I thought you and I were, you know, serious."

"We are. I *am*. I love you." Hill had turned to him and tried to smile but it was too much of an effort. "I'm more the Let's-Live-Together-a-Few-Months-and-See Committed."

"You must think I'm a crazy old man." Raymond Mack

49

was seated next to the aisle, jeans and a white bushy ponytail, his legs crossed at the knee, doodling with a thin felt-tipped pen in a spiral notebook. He was too big and long for his seat – not fat, really, just oversized. Raymond kept drawing calamity sketches, airplanes in flames, airplanes sinking into the ocean, passengers crowded together on a metal wing protruding from water and wave. He said to Hill, "What can I tell you? I'm a romantic. Who would've thought, right? Dying with you is better than dying alone."

"Your cancer situation has got you thinking too much about death, Ray. Didn't the doc say you shouldn't worry? The cancer will outlive you."

"What do doctors know?"

"—More than you, sugar. Stop being a worry wart."

Hillary felt these conversations bordered on the creepy, or maybe this was how older people thought but, hell, same-same.

"It's the boner pills," he'd told her. "Isn't that what's this about, why you're willing to hang out with me? The wonders of chemistry?" Mr. Angst.

"You are some riot," she said. "Modesty isn't a good fit for you."

That's the talk Hill remembers from the plane ride.

It's two days later now – twelve-thirty-nine in the afternoon – and Hillary Ann is wearing one of Raymond's pale blue work shirts and that's about it. Stunning thighs, for sure – her body stunning from what ever angle you choose. She already has a perfect tan from her ninety-nine dollar, twelve session, pre-summer sale at Joey's Tanning Hutch in Ardmore, Pa.

She can see the Bay of Biscay from the wide living room window, very beautiful panorama but also very gray. Cloudy days are all Hill has seen since coming to Spain.

Baby-Ray says the spring is like that – no tourists to

speak of but some truly depressing rainy-ass days, for sure. A trade, solitude for crap weather. Maybe depressed boarding on suicidal, if she thought about it. The stupid rain wouldn't quit.

Hillary can also see the Santiago de Compostela Cathedral. *It's scary beautiful,* she thinks, *so Gothic.* Ray once told her that some of the statues decorating the building are there to keep away the demons.

Their house keeper goes to Compostela Cathedral. She's an older Spanish woman named Fiorella. Hill thinks the old woman is a true beauty, an absolutely serene face, not a line anywhere. *Well maybe a little around the eyes. But who doesn't have that.* It's Fiorella who told her the apostle James is buried there. His remains were brought to the church after getting decapitated in Jerusalem. *Can you imagine? A beheading, for Godsake! Who does that? What person in their right mind? You can't think too much about this historical stuff without getting psychotic.* The whole head cutting thing is too primitive for her.

"That's how people did business in those days," Baby Ray said as their plane landed at the Santiago de Compostela. "If you have to die before your time, the best is still a sharp blade and a very strong guy.

"It's positively medieval."

"—Quick is quick, my love."

Their villa has cold slate floors and beige stucco walls. Hillary's favorite living room chair is here, a big forest green velour recliner. She loves curling herself into the heart of it, the warmth, the softness of it. Hillary is there now, a cup of lovely hot mocha coffee between her hands. Baby Ray's sketches and oils hang on every wall – twenty, maybe thirty of them. His pencil sketches of old people are the best. They're haunting, their eyes and their sweet wrinkled cheeks.

This is why I love you, Raymond. I see you in the eyes

of these people. I see how they take to you. Hillary doesn't understand why he'd doubt her love. Who would not fall in love with Raymond Mack after seeing his work? One favorite is a painting of old men siting outside a café, playing chess. She likes the jokes behind their eyes. Another one Hillary loves is a pencil drawing of children hiding behind their mother's skirts and peering out at each other.

Hillary is the one who told Baby Ray about Dr. Grigor Bolian. "The mushroom guy," she calls him. "He's the one you want, hon." They're in the bed, lights just turned off. This happened maybe a month, month and half ago – one of those mini talks before sleep. Raymond describes how Isaac Stalin totally destroyed Lili's chance to get on in this world.

"Yeah, you want the mushroom guy," Hill says again.

"You're Bolian is an assassin?"

"I believe so, yes."

She didn't "believe" so. She knew so. A hour after arriving in Santiago. Hillary had purchased a Beretta on the back-market. A two-toned Pico .380 semi-automatic, the most concealable handgun in the Beretta line, the deal arranged by a friend of a friend a week before she and Baby-Ray left for Spain. Hillary did this to protect herself and to protect her significant other. That would be Baby Ray.

You did not deal with someone like Bolian without a firearm.

"How do you know these things?" Raymond had said.

"You don't need to know everything, hon." She liked being a "Woman of Mystery" for him. She could tell he admired that. It kept him interested. It kept him amused. It got Baby Ray hard.

SOMETHING LIKE AN AFFAIR REMEMBERED

Glenside, Pennsylvania
February 13, 1987

"WHERE WERE ISAAC Stalin's parents that night?"
Margaret Ramirez isn't getting it. She's wearing another of her concealing Muumuus, an ankle-length denim one. The therapist isn't getting how parents can let a bunch of teenagers take over a home. What sort of people do that? No supervision, no nothing? Margaret says, "It's not your fault, dear. Please know I'm not saying that. All you did was show up. I'm, I dunno, curious, I guess."

"—Next door. I heard somebody saying Isaac's parents were next door, at the Cobb's." Lili's folded hands rest on the knee of her crossed legs. Her skinny teen self looking very lost in a white tee under a brown wool crew neck, her dark hair hiding her face, long tangled strands, skin pale enough for the dead. "Trudy was with me – Trudy Cobb, she's my best friend since I don't know when, maybe kindergarten, not that she helped me that night. A *real* friend would've helped me."

"People get scared," Margret says. "—Young people, especially.

"I got pushed into a *pool*, for godsake. It was December." Whine, whine, she can hear her hideous voice. *God, if I had a knife I'd stab myself in the chest.* "Look, Miss Ramirez, I was totally drenched, okay? It was cold, rainy, a horrible night. I saw her at the glass patio door

53

with the rest of them. With the rest of the jerks, those *ass*holes. I'm looking at her and thinking, 'What is wrong with you? Why aren't you angry at them? Why aren't you *doing* something?' I won't ever forgive her. *Ever.* She's supposed to be my friend and all, my *best* friend." Lili glances up at Margaret, a moment or two, before looking down at her folded hands again. And hesitantly, "...I-I went over there."

"Where, the Cobbs?"

"I cut through the backyard."

"You never told me that part," Margaret says.

Lili shrugs the way she does at home when she doesn't do the obvious. Like, yeah, fine, whatever. She'd remembered another incident from that awful night, the facts and feelings of it vanishing and reappearing again and again like something that doesn't know where to go. "Hey I forgot. People forget. You can't expect me to know every little thing right off."

"You're right," Margaret says. She looks down at her own folded hands propped on her belly, a basketball-sized swell beneath her denim dress. "So you go to the Cobbs to find Isaac's parents."

"—More or less, yeah."

"I don't follow 'more or less.' Doesn't a person either go or not go?"

"I *mean* my ear is aching. I can't *hear* anything. Already I can't hear. It's so cold I think the water in my ear must be frozen, or something. I dunno. There are, what-you-call it, circumstances. Going over to the Cobbs's isn't what this is about, anyway."

"I'm just trying to put it together."

Lili is ignoring the therapist. She wants to say what she has to say. Who cares whether Ms. Fatso is trying to 'put it together.' *How is that my problem?* "I'm in their backyard," Lili is saying, "—The Cobbs's backyard, and the basement light is on. I'm looking through one of the tiny windows, half in the bushes. It's really cold, you know? The wind, all the rain. I see Isaac's parents, the Cobbs, two or three other couples. The basement has a Christmas tree lit up, and colored lights are on the pine panel walls. They got a bar down there, too. Very Christmassy."

Margaret is about to speak but decides to wait and listen. The gray afternoon light is behind her, on the white office walls, the wood floor.

"I felt this blanket on my shoulders," Lili whispers. She could see herself in the backyard again, feel the warmth of the wool about her. "Then I hear Isaac, 'You're gonna freeze,' he tells me. 'C'mon now. Hey. C'mon.' He's trying to get me to clam down, that's what I thought. He even pats the blood from the cut I got above my right eye with his handkerchief. You know, when he pushed me in the pool. I smell the wine on him, that pukey smell. God, I absolutely hate that smell. Wine, whiskey, they all got a smell. But he's sounding very kind and all. It's, you know, shocking to me, that kindness."

"I'll take care of you," Isaac whispers.

"I can barely hear him. My stupid ears. And I'm not thinking good, you know? Lots of times I just don't think good, I don't do the thinking a person ought to do. 'I-I'm freezing,' I say. I'm afraid the chatter of my teeth are gonna unhinge my jaw. Never been so cold in my life."

'Let's go in here," Isaac says to me, very concerned, that's how it sounded. 'Out of the rain and stuff,' he says."

The boy took her into the small metal tool shed in the Cobbs's backyard – no heat, no floor but the hard, frozen ground. He rubbed her hair dry with the blanket. He took off her clothes, too. Like he was her mama and had her best interest first. But he wasn't her mama. Mamas don't have penises.

"Let me get this straight." Margaret sat up, smoothing

55

out her over-sized dress. "This boy – this Isaac – pushes you into the pool. Purposely, aggressively, pushes you. He shoves you into half filled pool of filthy water and what – logs? Was it logs? Didn't you say logs?"

"—To keep the water from freezing, yes."

"—*Germ* filled water." Margaret emphasizes the whole germ thing.

"—Yeah, at least. Squirrel shit and stuff."

"Then he does what – rape you?"

"No, *no*." Lili gave two quick waves of her hand. "He was *very* gentle. I'd never felt anything like that I my life – the sex, you know. I mean I've done stuff to myself, of course. Laid on my stomach and rubbed myself on the bed. Like that. But not sex with another person. That's what I want to say – *never* sex with another person. God, I didn't know anything could be so good." She glances at her therapist, a tiny nervous peek, then looks at her crossed knee. "He left so, I dunno, *fast*. Like I had the plague, or whatever. I wanted to tell him he could do it again, if he wanted. I wanted to do it again. I wanted him to hold me and keep me from getting cold."

THE NIGHT HILL MET GRIGOR

The Village
May 31ᵗʰ, 1996, Evening

WHEN HILLARY MET Grigor – she nineteen and he thirty-eight and still talking about what Reagan would do about all things – she felt both attracted and repelled by the man. She liked his formal yet flirty manner, his tailored, dark gabardine suit, the initials on his French cuffs. *Okay, sue me,* she'd thought at the time. She also liked that his hair was trimmed and nicely combed. *He had an elegance about him. People like elegance, don't they?* What brought them together was a party at Kara Nissim's Greenwich Village home to celebrate Bibi Netanyahu's election as Israel's new PM.

"He's their Reagan," Grigor said.

"Do we need another one?"

"We *always* need a patriot, dear."

He had the condescending little prick quality of a believer.

Kara's work as a clothing designer had begun receiving praise and the apartment had its share of trade types – "the screech and primp crowd," she called it.

Kara was also Armenian and a first cousin to Dr. Bolian's mother. Hillary had taken the woman's design class at NYU and they'd become friends. Kara knew everybody, what they did and who they did it with. She loved saying, *"Teaching and living in the Village will keep you eternally young, my darling!"* In '96 Kaka Nissim was becoming known for her cardigans, dusters, and Alpaca coats. That year browns and whites were in, particularly desert tans.

"You're a surgeon?" Hill said to Grigor. She was working on her third glass of red, a Pinot Noir.

"Does that sort of thing intrigue you?"

They were sitting on a silk pearl colored sofa in a shadowed corner of a living room filled with chatty people.

It did intrigue her. "How can you cut into a person?" She wanted to know.

"Oh that's the fun part."

"I think I would faint dead away."

"—Many do. In med school we were peeling them off the floor. Very amusing, really." Another one of his condescending, La-De-Da moments. *Why do I like this guy at all?* she thought. Then Grigor said, "The trick is, don't see them as human. Never, never, never. You see them as – how shall I say – fleshy machines."

"—Like Zombies." Hill was gazing into her wine glass.

"That's it, exactly. But anesthetized."

"—Wow. Like the Nick Lowe song."

"—The what?"

"You know, 'You got to be cruel to be kind.' It's an oldie., '78, '79, I think." Hill took another sip of her red. "I always thought the song gave everybody permission to mess with their friends. Like you're actually doing a good thing by fucking over this one or that one."

"*Ahhh,* I see." Grigor was nodding, grinning at her. *God, he had these perfect teeth, little but perfect.* "Interesting 'Cruel to be kind" – yes, that's it, very much it," he said. "I'll remember that one."

A day or two before the party Kara Nissim had told Hill how Grigor killed his father's brother. They were on the phone, eleven-thirty, twelve at night. Hillary was in bed watching that ancient Cary Grant-Deborah Kerr movie.

Kara is saying, "—Eighteen years old and he kills his uncle, his father's brother, that's what people say. Who knows, right? Obviously he got away with it. The father, Sako, he loved his son. Grigor could do no wrong in the eyes of the father. The boy would've done anything for the father. That part I'm sure of – many people have said this."

"So you're related to Grigor."

"I try not to think about it. But, yes."

Kara was mostly bones wrapped in wrinkled white skin. She had gray hair done in a buzz cut and little gold hoops outlined her right ear. Her clothes were black, a black T, black slacks, black Audrey Hepburn flatties. Hill thought people in the arts needed to broaden their color spectrum.

"The guy's sort of sexy, don't you think?" Hill said.

"You're such a bad girl." Kara's laugh turned into a cough. Hill could hear all that smoker's phlegm rumbling about the wall of her chest.

"Has he killed, you know, other people?"

"—Besides the uncle? It wouldn't surprise me. There are rumors, of course.

But there are also people who have a rich fantasy life." Kara fixed another cigarette into a small holder, using a silver lighter to get it going. "Why, my dearest? Have somebody in mind, do we?"

"I got a list." And quickly, "—Kidding."

"Don't we all."

LET THE PAIN BEGIN

The Pyrenees
April 12th, Later in the day

IT'S 487.7 MILES to Santiago de Compostela from St. Jean Pied de Port.

"Pacing is everything," Lili Mack says to Isaac. The two of them are beginning their climb over the Pyrenees. She's paraphrasing the guide book. One part Lili reads twice to herself before saying anything out loud. The book says they will go from two hundred meters above sea level to fourteen hundred meters before starting a very steep descent into the beech woods and then Roncesvalles. "The first day is supposed to be the hardest," she tells him. Talk about editing. *Why go into details?*

"How hard is hard?" he wants to know.

"They have health clinics in Logofio," she says, ignoring his question. "That's about a hundred and sixty kilometers from here. They treat leg and foot injuries. Good thing we got ole Logofio, huh?"

"—Wonderful."

"We can do this," she says.

"Hey. We're middle-aged, princess."

No arguing that one, Lili thinks. She also thinks, *What's with this 'princess' shit?*

Seriously. There are moments that she loves Isaac Stalin. There are also moments she wants to see him suffer in the worst way. She'd like to stick with one or the other and stop flipping back and forth.

The clouds are gray and black and hover low in a hard blue sky. Lili Mack and Isaac are walking on a dirt path and the hills around them and ahead of them are severe patches of light and dark green as the shadows from the clouds roll over the land.

"This isn't a race," Lili says. "That's what we have to keep in mind. Slow and steady, okay? Can we agree on that?" She looks at Isaac, only a second or two. Lili doesn't want to upset him so early on. "I mean that's what I do, you know? Everything for me is a competition, everything is a race. Oh it's true, you wouldn't know it to look at me." Self-degradation is the way to go. Lecture yourself and hope the person you're actually lecturing hears you. "I have to remind myself to work together with you. That you and I are a couple, a team."

"You can count on me," Isaac Stalin says. He says it with real conviction, real something – *resolve*. That's it – *resolve*. This boy means business. No sarcasm, no chuckles, no slanty-eyed scheming, no bullshit. "When I'm on board, I'm there all the way," he says. "No namby-pamby shit, not with *my* girl."

Great. Now I'm a forty-two year old 'girl.'

Lili thinks about Hillary's phone call, the one she got on her cell before the beginning of this pilgrimage. Lili didn't know what to make of Hillary Ann Tucker.

What thirty-something woman wants to get naked and have sex with a sixty-something man? Lili couldn't imagine her father wanting that, the humiliation alone would undo him.

"Your father hired a guy," Hill had said.

"What do you mean 'guy'?" Lili didn't get it, not at first.

"You know. A ... *guy*."

Lili Mack remembers feeling totally stupid. She'd been sitting cross-legged on her nylon blue sleeping bag, cell wedged between her shoulder and ear, stuffing the last items in her backpack, four small plastic baggies of almond - M&M trail mix. Then it dawns on her – *bam!* like an awakening – *Assassin. Isn't that it? God my father hired a gangster.*

The idea did not completely offend her.

"...how did you know?" Lili whispered.

"We discuss things. I told him about a guy, an acquaintance."

I never believed he was serious. She had thought all that talk was her father being upset about his cancer thing. *You churned up a whole fantasy about me and my 'lost potential' – whatever that is – but it's really about you, isn't it, daddy? What you'll leave behind, how you'll be remembered. You can't even see how scared you are. Oh you'll die all right, but not any time soon and it won't be from some dumb prostate.*

"—I-I didn't actually give my okay," Lili said to Hill.

"Easy, I like you. I wanted to give you a heads up."

Their talk lasted no more than five or so minutes.

Lili is still thinking about her father's girlfriend as Isaac Stalin takes her attention with complains about the rain. They aren't even close to fourteen hundred meters up the Pyrenees and the man can't keep it together. It's raining in some spots but not other spots and Isaac is talking about the rain following him. Like it's personal.

"Pretend you're a duck," Lili says.

"—What?"

"Ducks love rain."

"Are you fucking *serious*?"

"...quack, quack," she said, mostly to herself.

God, was this a mistake.

WHATEVER UNIVERSE HE REVOLVES AROUND NOW

Philadelphia
March 17th, Less than a month ago

LILI MACK RECOGNIZES the heavy breathing but says, "Okay, who *is* this." Saying it, anyway. Like let's check the extensive list of men who insist on calling her at two and three in the morning. "Men" not "man" – *imagine* – like she's gone viral. Her life as a YouTube video. Only it's two men, really. Isaac Stalin and this one, her ex, the self-flagellating Norman Pearlman, the astrophysicist, Dr. Dark Matter himself. Lili and Norm were in their late-twenties when they divorced, a marriage impulsively begun and wearily escaped, both instigated by Lili, her hubby no more than a deer in her headlights. Now he's married to an obese Filipino and lives with her and her four Ritalin enhanced children from a previous marriage in Vermont. Yes, Freeze-Your-Knees Vermont.

"You know who this is?" He always begins with that.

No, Norm, who is it.

He doesn't wait for an answer. "It's Dr. Norman Pearlman," he says. And just so she doesn't confuse him with some other Dr. Norman Pearlmans, he says, "—Your ex."

"Oh *that* Norman Pearlman."

Silence. Then he says, "I miss your sense of humor."

"Uh-huh. How 'bout my pussy?"

"—Another joke, right?"

Dr. Norm wouldn't know humor if it came up and gave

him a blow job.

FYI: the first time Lili gave him a blow job, he'd said, "Thank you, dear. Very nice." Like she had given him a pair of argyles for whatever, Chanukah.

The digital clock reads 2:10 AM. An empty bottle of chardonnay is beside the clock on the nightstand. Next to the bottle is a partially filled wine glass with a smear of cherry red gloss on the rim.

"What brings you to these parts," she says, thinking how western that sounds, how very John Ford.

"I've had one of my premonitions." This used to be a big thing in their marriage.

The occasional premonition offered up by the background hum of the Big Bang, or the way star clusters had formed.

That's the other thing about her ex-hubby that troubles her. Dr. Norm believes the universe presented him with special knowledge, say, the ability to see into the distant and the not-too-distant future, the ability to give warnings to friends and loved ones.

"You heard I was dating someone?" she says. Guessing.

"I never pass judgment."

The schoolmarm is right again.

"I'm a single person now," Lili says, groggy and feeling a little defensive. She doesn't bothering opening her eyes. "Our marriage vows have been ... declassified." *No, that's not it. What the hell is the word?* Oh whatever you'd call it – freed ... *unchained.* I'm no longer bound to you, Norm. You know, Big-Girl-on-Her-Own, that sort of thing."

"You'll always be my Lili."

"Tell that to the Filipino."

"—Samoan."

"Whatever. How's the missus and all the little Samoans?"

"I was talking to Raymond last weekend," Dr. Norm says, avoiding her cynicism. That's the other thing. The ex-hubby keeps apprised of her business through the Chatty Cathy father. Norm says, "— My God, Lili, cancer of the prostate? Why can't you pick up a phone and tell me? You *do* realize I'm the one who made you and Raymond rich? Rather, my wife's expertise in stocks. Her sug*gest*ions. But I *am* the faithful messenger. The least you could do is keep me in the loop. Why withhold such heartbreaking information?"

His wife is a psychologist and stock market savant.

"I don't know." Lili breaths an audible sigh. "Because it's none of your business? Yes, that must be it. Wait, wait, let me think about this." Pause. "Yes, because it's none of your business."

"You've always rejected the people who care the most."

"—Norman."

"...yes?"

"You and I are done." Very clearly articulated.

"Oh *God*," Dr. Norman whispers the Lord's name and pauses before saying, "What's a person supposed to do with you?"

"—Excuse me?"

"I *said*—"

"Yeah, Norm, I know what you said." Now Lili is wide awake and fantasizing what could kill this man in the slowest, most agonizing way possible – something with screams attached. "Leave my father alone," Lili says, shutting her eyes tight. "Leave *me* alone, you creepy little fuck. Leave our *family* alone. Leave our friends alone. Leave the people who you think we might get to know in the future alone."

"The night after talking to your father, I had my premonition." Dr. Norman hears what he wants to hear. All comments that don't go along with his personal scenarios have a way of vanishing. That's always been his way. He has probably dismissed Lili's talk as a PMS rant or another chemical thing that has nothing to do with the rational part of her. He says, "Woe will befall you, Lili."

"Norm, did you just use the word 'woe'?"

"Woe will befall you and yours." he says again.

"Good to hear from you, Norm."

MR. STALIN HAS A MAN-TO-KID WITH LITTLE ISAAC

Broad and Olony, Philly
December 24ᵗʰ, 1987

"YOU WANT THIS fucking cello thing, or what?" His dad's saying that.

"—Yeah, I want it." Isaac's voice is a bit louder than a whisper.

He's fifteen years old, a lagging eleventh grader, all bones and pale skin. His year off with rheumatic fever doesn't help the vision his father has of him. He's seen as a bright but sickly kid. Family physician, Dr. Nickolas Kormos, demands that the boy receive penicillin shots until his twenty-first birthday.

"I can't hear you." Mr. William Stalin. cups his right ear with a slender hand.

He's wearing his English tweed and a Joseph Abboud charcoal and pink paisley tie, the knot a four in hand. Father and son are driving down Broad Street in the father's silver Chrysler Fifth Avenue, the December day cold and cloudless, heading to Center City and the father's investment firm on Walnut Street. Mr. Stalin, says, "You must learn to speak up. You must *take* the world, William, no one will give it to you. Being sick forever isn't an option. Where is this school, again?"

"—The Casaux in Madrid."

"Ah, Spain. Very good, very classy. Your taste is my taste, excellent. Again, let me ask. Do *you*, William, want this fucking cello thing?"

"Yes, I *want* it. Okay? I *want* it."

"I believe you, William. I believe you want the cello thing. But what are you willing to do to get it?"

"Play well," the boy says, thinking this is the right answer, the sort of son's answer a father could appreciate, a Got-My-Shit-Together answer. "—No, play *perfectly*.

I've been practicing three, four hours a day. Yesterday my fingers were bleeding. Or one of them, my middle finger."

"Every kid will be doing that," his father says. "Every kid's middle finger will be bleeding. Playing well is what people *do* at your level. Trust me." William is more than unimpressed. He's bored. He yawns and covers his mouth briefly with his manicured fingertips. "I expected a better plan from you."

"I-I don't understand."

Isaac thinks playing his best is always a fine plan. This is what his mother tells him. Ramona Stalin says to do his very best and not to worry about anyone else. His mom is a small, quiet person – five-two, five-three, very petite – and she likes leather coats of all types and styles. She also likes keeping her nails filed just-so and painted, either red or lavender.

"You must step outside the box," William tells his son. "Do you know that expression – 'outside the box'? Have we ever discussed that, the idea of stepping away from what is proper, the morays of the ordinary?"

A muddy Ford pickup cuts in front of William. William and the Ford 150 trade angry honks. "—Asshole," the old man hissing at the Ford.

"Will you help me?" Isaac doesn't know what else to say.

His father takes an audile breath, an attempt to regain focus. "I know nothing about the arts," he says. "*But* – I do know about winning. I know what a person must do to win. The arts are no different than any other business, son. You must have what we call a P. O. A. – a Plan of Attack. Something ruthless, something that will cut your enemy at the knees. Perhaps 'enemy' is too evocative a phrase. Opponent. Yes, bring your *opponent* to his knees. Now that I think about it, 'ruthless' is also too harsh. Let's use 'dedicated,' okay? You must dedicate yourself to bringing your opponent to his knees."

"—Her knees," Isaac says. "It's a girl."

"Oh, a *girl*?" finds this humorous. "How good is the girl?"

"—Very good. You should hear her do Bach's Prelude."

"Is the girl as good as you? Be honest." His father glances at him then looks back at the Center City traffic. "You're good, right? On a scale of one to ten, what are you? An Eight? A nine?"

"—Eight maybe."

"—*Eight*? Do you know how many nines and tens there are?" has gone from being amused to being shocked. "In *everything*? The world is run by nines and tens and you're tell me you're an eight?"

"Occasionally, I'm a nine." Isaac is good but not as good as Lili Mack. He's known that for awhile. Definitely, a ten, Lili Mack. When the boy listens to Lili play, he admires her and hates himself. "There are, you know, different *types* of good."

"A person's either good or they aren't," Mr. Stalin says.

"I play as good as I can, okay? I'm good."

"But the girl is better."

"Nobody can make another person play worse," Isaac says.

"Then you must change her itinerary."

"—Do what?"

"—Change her plans."

ON THE ROAD WITH THE DOCTOR

Medina
April 12th, Late afternoon

THERE ARE sand-colored castles in Medina and the churches have domes and tall gothic spires. The rain has come and gone but the gray streets are still wet and the sun is low in the sky and the yellow light goes between the clouds. In the cafés, the wine suggested is *Castalo de Medina Verdejo*. A 2013, if they have it. Dr. Grigor Bolian has just passed the Café Cantones with its tan and white awning and small whicker tables and chairs. *What's with Spain and all the wine?* he's thinking, and smiles to himself. *Is it the bullfights? Who doesn't need a drink after a bullfight? Bulls forfeit their lives so the depressed tourists will order another glass of Verdejo, '13.*

People are returning to the streets and the markets. This skimpy sort of rain is never a game changer for anyone.

"Such a lovely day," the man says. He is in his late thirties. Men do not talk to Grigor unless they want to sell him something or fuck him. Since he neither buys nor fucks them, they're always disappointed.

"You are a man of integrity," The Commander whispers to Dr. Bolian, that head wobbling, Reaganesque voice. The doctor feels a warmth emanating from his own chest, a sense of calmness. The Commander has been steady and very supportive throughout this trip. *"We must refrain from these degenerate life styles, men with men,*

73

women with women, yet we must keep our disgust to ourselves. We need to get along, find a kind word for each of God's creatures – no matter how it repels us. This is the American way. What makes our country great."

"It is a lovely day, isn't it?" The doctor says. He's supposed to meet his employer in Madrid, a couple of hours ago now. But it's too glorious a day for it. He is wandering the market. In front of him are two wooden troughs, one filled with olives and the other filled with sunflowers. When Dr. Bolian turns to looks at the man, he is taken by his pale skin and the delicate veins along his arms and legs. The man's faded denim shorts look very new, perhaps a person who'd like to fit in but isn't used to being a tourist. His face has a washed out appearance, a weary sort of quality, someone too tired to put himself together in a crisp manner. "You're from where in America?" Grigor says.

"—Vermont."

"—Ahhh. Of course." *Not miserable, just Vermont.* "—What part?"

"Kettledrum. It's a small town."

Before looking about the market, Dr. Bolian had been pondering the woman he'd left at the Hotel de Peregrino in Pamplona. Jessie Cole was a shrieker of operatic proportions. Who would've thought he'd almost lacked the patience to let the mushroom tea do its job? He did, of course, let the mushrooms work. But it was touch and go. It would've been so much easier to just stab the bitch and be finished with it. She was well on her way to her grand finale when he left her.

Another illustration of how he must work on his flaws. *"All Americans have our 'trouble areas,' areas we must improve,"* The Commander murmurs. *"These imperfections reflect our humanity. It's a quality people from all over our great planet admire in us – that*

American Can-Do Spirit. Yes, we are close to perfect, no doubt about it. But can't we do better? Can't we strive – like Don Quixote fighting his windmills – to be as close to perfection as we can achieve? To say as Don Quixote said, 'I know who I am and who I may be, if I chose.' Isn't this the true American spirit?"

He had watched her vomit.

When you're wrong you're wrong. *No one's perfect. Sorry, my Commander. I should have stabbed the bitch. Put her down quick. No suffering, no building up a huge reservoir of hatred before leaving this life. What's that saying? 'Hindsight is always twenty-twenty,' something like that.*

Ms. Cole wasn't ashamed of vomiting over everything. She wasn't ashamed of begging right up to the end. He'd hoped the people next-door thought they were having great sex.

Forget this. What done is done.

"...I'm a lawyer," the man from Vermont is telling him, the depressed blond.

"My name's Wheatfield. Jake Wheatfield. I have a card here somewhere." The man is already patting down various pockets.

Grigor Bolian pretends to study the card.

Jonathan E. Wheatfield, Esq.

Attorney at Law.

What's to study, really – a name, a couple of telephone numbers, an address the doctor doesn't know? Fine. He's a lawyer. *Obviously the man's both a lawyer and a good detective.*

Grigor tucks the card away.

"They pay your way here, Mr. Wheatfield?" the doctor says. "—Your client? I hope you got a first class ticket."

"Please, call me Jake."

"—Fine," Grigor says. "Jake it is. How did you fine me

Jake?"

"My client is a person who does what it takes." Jake removes a photo and hands it to Grigor. "Remember this one?"

Grigor does. It's half of a picture taken years ago – in New York, the Village.

The missing half was of a woman he'd known years ago, Hillary somebody. Tucker.

Yes, Hillary Tucker.

"Where did you get this," Dr. Bolian wants to know.

"My client has many friends, mutual acquaintances."

"—Apparently. So you've been – what – stalking me?"

"I'm good at my job," Jake says. He nods toward the Café Cantones. "I was about the have a glass," he says. "I want to try that *Castalo de Medina Verdejo*. It just sounds so tasty."

"—*Ahh*, very tasty. Excellent choice, counselor."

"People love the *Verdejo*."

"—When in Spain." Dr. Bolian gives him a grin. "My lady friend is forever saying, 'If you're going to Medina you must taste the *Verdejo*.' You know women. Am I right?" The doctor doesn't have a lady friend but no sense having an awkward moment.

Then Bolian says, "Am I wrong to think your client and I are interested in many of the same people?"

"—Enough similarities to bring me here," Jake says.

Grigor holds out a hand toward one of the Cantone's outside wicker tables, an After-You gesture. "Please don't get the wrong idea. I've never been much of a drinker."

"—Who is, sport."

After two glasses of the *Verdejo* and comments on the nightmares and humor of travel, Jake Wheatfield got to the point.

"—My client has an offer," the lawyer says.

Dr. Bolian already had a guess or two but let Jack go

on.

"Ten thousand more than your current contractor," Jake Wheatfield says as he watches two girls walking through the market on the opposite side of the narrow street, both college age, both wearing baseball caps and backpacks. One is a skinny blonde, the other is field hockey material. Jack says, "—Eighty-five thousand. That's ten thousand more than your current employer."

"I've no idea of what 'employer' you're discussing." Grigor poured some of the *Verdejo* into his own glass. He takes a quick sip, returning the glass to the wicker table and says, "What does one do for eighty-five K these days? Just out of curiosity."

"Anything my client tells you to do."

WOES OF THE PILGRIM

Larrasoana
April 13th, Present

ON THE SECOND day of their hike, Isaac Stalin trips and falls, a graveled area near the side of a road. He tears some skin and flesh off his right knee. Lili has a first aid kit with bandages and antiseptic in her blue nylon backpack. They are a kilometer or so outside Larrasoana.

"You come prepared," he says, watching as she cleans his wound.

"It's genetic. My mom was a nurse."

"Thank God or mom." No sarcasm, the guy is relieved.

There are ancient stone bridges in Larrasoana, and cattle feed on the grasslands. Narrow medieval streets and one and two story stone houses with big wood doors are everywhere. If you injure yourself, this is a decent enough place to do it. The café Bar Larrasoana has a polished wood bar and a fine collection of whiskeys. Villagers call it the pilgrim's bar. Outside the bar near the wood chairs and the little wood tables, an old man and a boy play with a red cape. It is the Spanish pastime of boys who have dreams and old men who've dreamt and still dream.

"How is it?" Isaac wants to know, meaning his wound.

"Not so good, but no need for stitches."

"How 'bout my quality of life?"

There is a one or two second pause before Lili gets that he's joking. Isaac Stalin is one of those serious, straight-faced jokers. At first you think he's all somber and out of it, but the more you're around him the more she has a sense of him, the way he goes about things.

"Hey, this is a step up for you," she says, mimicking

his delivery.

Off and on Lili's thinks about Norman Pearlman's premonitions. Dr. Norm, her space cadet Ex. Her Samoan crazed, good-hearted ex. Or at least, well-meaning. In a weird way she has missed Dr. Norm. The men in her life have always been self-absorbed but far from dumb, including the original man, the proto-type of all men – Lili's daddy, Raymond Mack. That's what Margaret Ramirez would say. Parents are templates for who we judge, pick or reject others. *"We are learning machines,"* she will tell you over and over. *"Everything is either mommy or daddy."* Margaret liked to ask Lili what memories this man or that one invoked. Most times Lili didn't recall anything.

"Woe will befall you, Lili."

What was she supposed to make of that? Did Norman expect her to call off her trip? He reminded her of a fortune teller in a silent movie. *The man's a drama queen.* Dr. Norm did that in their marriage, too. He'd wake her after one of his dreams and tell her crazy shit. *"Take the subway today,"* he would whisper. Or, *"Stay away from tuna."*

Two in the morning. For three months she didn't eat tuna. In those days she took him seriously, so it was impossible to know if he was ever right or wrong.

"Woe will befall you, Lili."

She has pictured Dr. Pearlman with his students at the Kettledrum College Observatory in Vermont. Seekers. Explorers. The bunch of them gazing into the star-pricked black for clues. According to Norm, that's how he did it – his predictions. He'd look at the stars through a telescope and *"...let them form images. That's all I do, Lili. I let the stars talk to me."* The universe was Dr. Norm's personal Rorschach Test.

Isaac wrapped his arm about Lili's shoulder. Her arm

circles his waist. He's hobbling along next her, a sort of fast moving hop. Her wounded little soldier. The Way of the Pilgrim is grim with the unexpected. They take a shortcut through a big meadow. Brown and white cows are grazing there. Isaac actually tells her to stop so he can pet a cow. This particular cow right away raises its head and the little soldier gets anxious and wants to hobble on. When Isaac finally sees the Café Bar Larrasoana, he hobbles faster and Lili tell him to slow the fuck down, for God-sake.

"I need a drink," he says.

"—*You* need a drink."

FUN WITH MUSHROOMS

Medina
April 13th, Late morning

"**T**HAT'S AN ENORMOUS spider, don't you think?" Jake Wheatfield says this to Dr. Bolian, nodding toward the center of the tan wicker table. It's ten-twenty in the morning and Bolian and Wheatfield are back at the Café Cantones, the same outside table as yesterday, except today Dr. Bolian is eighty-five thousand dollars richer, the money in his off shore account. Jake is saying, "Look at that big fury thing. Holy cow, seriously, what type of spider is it? Like a Tarantula? Is it like that, Grigor? Is it one of those – I dunno, fuckin' what-ya-call it – Tarantulas?"

Nothing is there, of course. Nada. Zip.

"Looks pretty friendly," Dr. Bolian says.

"—Fury monster bitch, if you ask me."

When Wheatfield had gone to the restroom, Grigor dumped a small envelope of *Copelandia mexicana* into the lawyer's breakfast *Verdejo*. That was close to an hour ago.

"You need more wine," Dr. Bolian says. "Nothing like a glass of wine to calm the soul, my friend." There was no reason to put a hallucinogenic in Jake's drink except for its entertainment value. Pretty damn funny, if you ask the doc.

"*I've always found you Amusing,*" The Commander whispers. "*—You and the very popular Rich Little. Funny, funny. Americans are known for their clever wit, their perceptive cultural insights. And we are the first to find ourselves amusing. Americans have always made the world laugh.*"

Wheatfield could've been freezing to death the way he was shaking. The doc says, "So who's my benefactor, counselor? Who do I thank for such generosity?"

Jake giggles; wags a finger. "No can do, no can do, buddy. Attorney-client, you know. But what a clever boy, you are. Yes, sir. Yes, siree-bob. You know all about that and you still want to know."

"—'Bout what?" Grigor says, total innocence.

"—*Privilege.* Client-Attorney privilege." Jake Wheatfield has become coy. Dr. Bolian swears the guy just batted his eyes. Counselor is like a teenage girl guarding her new tits. The man says, "I wish I could, Grigor. May I call you Grigor?" No waiting for an answer. "I'd certainly thank anyone who gave me that much money. It's the human thing to do, isn't it? What your decent people do. And anyone can see you are just that, Greg – a very decent guy."

"Thanks, Jake."

"—No problems."

"This is precious," The Commander mutters. Dr. Bolian can barely hear the man, though he gets the sense of it, that Hollywood-cowboy drawl. *"I used to do this exact same bob-and-weave with my bosses at Warner Brothers. What sons-of-bitches. You cut their dicks off, if you can. After all, they'd do the same to you. It's the way of the world, what we do here in America. And let there be no mistake, we do it better than anyone else, my boy. We know how to cut off a dick, believe me."*

Grigor pours more *Verdejo* into the lawyer's almost empty glass.

The morning is chilled and the sky has smeary clouds. A mist permeates the air. Everything feels damp. A fat woman with bib-apron and dyed orange hair has just placed a wood tray of sausages and hot, uncut bread between the two men. The smell reminds Bolian of Jersey in the summer, the hamburgers and fries at Wildwood.

"Just so we're clear, what does your guy want for his money?" Grigor fills his own glass with the *Verdejo*.

"We've already spoken on this," the lawyer says.

"I'm the eccentric type. Tell me again."

"They walk away."

"I have to show something, some effort," Dr. Bolian says. He is thinking about Raymond Mack's seventy-five thousand.

"My client isn't unreasonable. A wound is fine, a substantial wound is never frowned upon, Greg. Something that says you tried and almost succeeded. My client doesn't want you losing that seventy-five K."

"—Grigor."

"—What?"

"—My first name. It's *Grigor*." The doctor has pulled off a small chunk of the warm bread and is coating it with butter. He likes the knife – sharper than the usual, longer, too. It reminds him of one of his own antique surgical knives, a collector's item, a Jacob J. Teufel, *circa* 1870s.

Jake grins, teeth yellowed slightly, probably a smoker in rehab. "Americans like to get chummy far too quickly, don't we? No offense."

"Just so you know the name."

"Oh absolutely. Apologies to you and yours."

Dr. Bolian is wishing he'd given the lawyer a double dose of the *Copelandia mexicana*, enough to stop the condescending little bastard's heart. He also reminds himself to have another look at the photos that Raymond Mack had given him of his daughter and the Stalin guy.

A good assassin knows his targets and his contracts.

Rain taps on the tan and white awning above them. The light, irregular beat has no rhythm. Colorful umbrellas have bloomed along the gray narrow street and the market opposite Café Cantones, umbrellas hiding the faces of tourists.

"Suppose I accidently eliminate the target," Grigor says, mostly to amuse himself.

"You know, one of those 'woops' moments. After all, shit does happen."

"Then you've not lived up to your end of the contract." The lawyer sniffs the wine. Perhaps he's noticed the ever-so-slight bitter taste the *Copelandia mexicana.* "The contract says the funds transferred to your account would then be returned to us. Only fair, don't you think."

"Say I'd given it my best."

"—Admirable." Jake smiles and takes another sip of the *Verdejo.* "We appreciate an employee who does his best. We expect the employee to do so."

"...but?"

"Why go there, doctor."

Interesting, Bolian thinks. *Leave the consequences to my imagination. I like that, horrors limited only by what I can pull from my ass.*

Grigor rises from his chair as he is patting the corners of his mouth with a white linen napkin. "Please excuse," he says. "I've another appointment, but do thank your employer for me." Jake is looking at the table top and doesn't speak. *Probably another spider*, Bolian thinks. *The guy loves his spiders.* He's behind the lawyer when the blade comes out, something sharper and longer than a butter knife. Grigor runs the knife across the left side of Wheatfield's neck, cutting the carotid artery then walks away.

Immediately Jake is slumped nap-like on the table. His blood has already begun to spread across the wicker top, seeping through the grooves of the weave, dripping onto the stone floor of the café's patio.

THE GRAND LADY OF MANY STARS

Kettledrum College Observatory
Kettledrum, Vermont

MOST OBSERVATORIES DON'T have heat. If they happen to have heat, the observer can't use it because it fogs the lens. Now add a few other issues. Kettledrum Observatory is on top of a 4,439 foot Mountain called Mt. Icarus. And you work at night.

And you work in nut freezing Vermont. Dr. Norman Pearlman likes to say if he'd known about the heat-cold-mountain-night thing from the start, he would have probably become a theoretical physicist in a warm office with a wall-sized white board and lots of felt-tip pens.

"...the ancient Egyptians used the stars to guide their lives," Dr. Norm is saying.

It's his two in the afternoon graduate seminar, obsessive note takers all. His attention is divided today. He's been obsessing a lot about his ex, Lili Mack. *How do I get Lili to believe she's heading into a dangerous time, especially on a dumb premonition.* Then he says to his students, "Of course, we can't ignore the sky goddess, Hathor, can we? She is known as The Lady of the Stars. Some call her, "Queen of the Milky Way.""

One of the note takers snickers.

Ho-ho yourself, you little bastard, Dr. Norm thinks and scans the half-dozen or so young faces for clues. But nothing, not a blip of a smile from any of them – *cowards. Any would be astronomer that doesn't appreciate intergalactic folklore isn't ready for the magnitude of the task.*

"God, where was I?" he mutters.

"—Queen of the Milky Way." Another snicker. *Ah, one of the gentlemen. You earth bound a-hole.* Dr. Norm does a second quick look, but these particular students are too smart for their own good.

"In one form or another, Hathor was worshiped throughout western Asia." He is still glancing about the room as he talks.

Here's the problem with being simply a theoretical physicist. Dr. Norm *adores* astronomy. Norm wears silk ties that have little moons and stars on black or navy blue backgrounds. He's a guy who smokes a pipe because Edwin Hubble smoked a pipe. He does *not* tell the others that he smokes a pipe because Hubble smoked a pipe but people know. People aren't dumb. To do what astronomers do is like being on meth without the rotten teeth. How wonderful to do this job, this *duty*, how extraordinary. Every night Norm Pearlman gets to open up the ceiling and watch the universe. Yes, *that* universe, the one that began thirteen billion years ago and has no end.

Let me repeat that: Has. No. End.

"Think of it," he says, pausing before he goes on and hoping the note takers will contemplate *some*thing. "The universe sprang out of *not* a 'singularity' but something very dense and hot, much smaller than what the Universe is now, a sort of space-time foam." Dr. Norm is feeling edgy, a bit paranoid.

Who is this snickering thorn in my side?

He goes on, "The universe is *not* curved. It is not like the inside of the proverbial balloon. No, the universe is an *end*less thing held together with dark matter and spurred onward by dark energy. Oddly, we don't know what any of that *is*, but we do know what it *does* – a sort of mobile scaffolding." Pearlman stopped and looked at his grad students who have yet to quit their note taking. He inhales an audible breath. "So. Tell me, dear people, isn't that reason enough to pursue astronomy?"

Nothing.

Are you kidding me?

Dr. Norm has left the goddess Hathor for the real world, or at least the world the note takers might feel comfortable inhabiting. He has counted seven Ph.D. students. They are seated about a dark horseshoe-shaped table – four young men, three young women. There is a burgundy and white oriental throw rug over a pine floor. Very, what people used to call, "Yuppie." Bleached pine.

Who does bleached pine, anymore?

"The *thing* appears out of *nothing*," Dr. Norm says. Why is irony difficult for young people? "Our incredibly, I dunno what adjective to use, how 'bout '*inexplicable*' universe. In*explicable*! And this galactic blooming appears out of its soupy foam and unfolds at a phenomenal rate, and *then* – as if to put a cherry on it – goes on *forever*. Everything. Every inch of it. Everything folds out – *bam!* – all at once."

Why, why, why!

How does this happens? What are its mechanisms? What makes it work, what is it for? Is that even an intelligent question?

More importantly, and don't we all know this is the bottom line, are there any more at home like YOU, like US?

The seven grad students continue writing their notes. No one is looking up. Dr. Norm glances at them before turning to the orange-red embers in the fireplace. April in Vermont is still damn cold, the sort of cold a person can feel under his skin, something buried in the bone.

A fireplace in a conference room, it boarders on the

romantic.

Lili Mack steps into his mind, again. She is shrouded in a blurred darkness. Her arms are stretched toward him, her expression wide-eyed, frantic.

"I remember our phone conversation – what you told me," she says, that Lauren Bacall thing she does. *"Why didn't I pay you the respect you deserved?"*

She will never thank him, of course. She will never know her caring ex has saved the life of her friend, Isaac Stalin, the twit cello player. Dr. Norm is not spending a small fortune to win his Lili back, or to have her regret an irresponsible decision, or to get a nice pity fuck. He is there only to serve, only to give her what she wants.

If the pity fuck happens – fine.

He returns to the seminar.

"—No thoughts? No questions?" Dr. Norman Pearlman doesn't get it. He tightens the rubber band that keeps his graying ponytail in place. When Norman started going bald, he started growing his hair on the sides and back. His Samoan wife, Moana, who is also a Vermont licensed clinical psychologist, calls it "Over compensation."

Is there any other kind?

Moana comes from new money. Her father passed on last year from a frontal lobe aneurism and the will divided the money from his restaurant chain, Luapo Fiso Noodle Delights – "Fast, Good Food Coast to Coast" – between her and her older brother, Afato, who tried suing her three times for the whole enchilada or, in her departed father's case, the Whole-Wheat Pasta with Tofu and Cucumber.

Dr. Norm is watching his students. *Young people, nothing stirs them. They're polymorphically anesthetized.* He could cut his wrists and bleed-out right in front of this bunch and no one would stop taking notes. No one would smell the blood and/or respond to the thud of his short, meaty body against the oriental rug or bleached pine floor. No one would put first dibs on his new black Reebok Work Tiahawks. Yet pens and pencils would pause in mid-air. One of them might eventually say, *"Do you think we'll have class tomorrow?"*

But that'd be about it.

Norm Pearlman is feeling his expanding universe slowly deflate.

"Pens down," Dr. Norm says. Immediately all pens collapse to the sides of their respective notebooks. Each student is looking at him, three young women, four young men. It has a Stepford Wives vibe. He says to them, "Why astronomy? Why not – oh I dunno – an MBA, or something in English literature?"

"...I like working at night," One of the young men says. This one has a thin, tan face and the perpetual beginning of a goatee. "It's quiet. It's not like working at K-mart or a law firm or – sorry, doc – teaching. I-I don't know how you do it."

"With all the love in my heart," Dr. Norm says.

What Norman Pearlman doesn't share with the boy and the other students is how he can channel the goddess Hathor. *All right, maybe 'channel' is a little creepy,* he thinks. *But it's definitely something.*

Years ago – we're talking '98, '99 – after many hours of looking at the night sky, Dr. Norman noticed that the stars had a tendency to form images. Or rather his mind had a tendency to give *meaning* to their random formations. His very own Psychologist-wife, Moana, likes to describe his talent as – "The personalization of the absolutely disinterested."

Lately the stars have given him the image of a cello. Dr. Norm is sure the cello shape is about his ex-wife, Lili Mack – lovely, sweet Lili who saved his life, Lili who stopped her Honda and walked down that snowy ditch to his bumped-off-the-road wreck, pulled open the passenger door and dragged him out. Did he mention minutes later the gas tank caught a spark and exploded? Like an end of the Earth sound. The pine above the blast had caught fire and the flames and the smell of burning sap filled the clear night sky.

Along with the heavens revealing a cello, he'd seen another image, so precise he found it on the Internet, a long dark-handled knife. The website showed antique surgical instruments. Dr. Norm believes the knife he saw was created by Jacob J. Teufel, *circa* 1870s.

ON THE ROAD TO SALVATION

Zubiri,
April 14th, Mid-day

"THERE'S A FREE Wi-Fi at the pilgrim hostel," Lili says, looking at the guide book.

"I'm sans iPad," Isaac Stalin says, prodding the dirty bandage on his right knee and wincing. "—I think I'm infected, maybe gangrene."

No, he's not dying of gangrene, Lili is pretty sure. The wound would be far more swollen and have a black-greenish color and the boy wouldn't be smelling all that great. This morning the skin just looks angry. She'd used an ink pen to dot the circumference of the surrounding red part, a way to judge the spread of the inflammation that signals an infection. Lili imagined Mom-the-Nurse being totally proud.

The irony of Isaac Stalin *actually* dying of gangrene doesn't escape her.

Halfway between Roncesvalles and Pamplona is Zubiri. It's a very small town known for its gray medieval bridge that goes over the Rio Arga. Some of the roads have white dust and some gray tar. The roads are narrow and don't go anywhere, or nowhere Lili can figure. A lot of dirty white stucco homes and ancient buildings in the town, most with shutters, and most of the shutters are rust colored.

"Why do you look so nervous?" Isaac wants to know.

"I'm *not* nervous."

"Hey I know nervous."

She is waiting for the assassin her father's girlfriend, Hillary, told her about, the guy who's supposed to kill Isaac. *Hillary's suggestion, by the way,* Lili can't grasp the idea. What sort of person tells the father about an assassin to kill the daughter's "friend" then tells the daughter to be on the watch for her suggestion. *You know why you're here,* Lili thinks. *Isn't it better to know than to be surprised?*

And surprises suck, some more than others.

"Are you worried about my condition?" Isaac says.

"—You're what?"

"—My leg, the wound."

"You don't have a condition, Isaac. It's a scraped knee."

They are on a dirt road surrounded by very green trees and overgrown grass. Lili walks. Isaac grunts and limps. She can see the town of Zubiri from here. It's about a half mile away. Rain appeared earlier in the morning but stopped an hour or so ago, the sky gray with big tattered clouds.

"I'm still betting you're nervous about my knee." He's already formed his own hypothesis and he's not giving it up. "You don't kid me, Ms. Mack."

"Wow. You really live in an opera."

"I'd be, you know, concerned about *you.*"

Ahhh, Lili got that. *"If you care about me, you'd be concerned,"* that's what he was saying, or what Lili thought he was saying.

"Yeah, you're right, Isaac. I'm concerned."

"—See."

"What can I say," Lili says, weariness in her voice. "You're a man who fathoms the human heart."

"Uh-huh. You bet your ass."

When was Hill's assassin guy going to kill him? *God, it*

couldn't be soon enough. Now you don't mean that. You couldn't possibly. Lili did not like to think of herself as a callous sort of person. She cried at old movies. She loved photos of kittens on YouTube and Facebook, particularly when they wore little costumes. *How's he gonna do it,* Lili wonders. *Sniper stuff? One of those rifles with a telescope thingie. 'Thingie?' Seriously? 'Telescopic Sight', okay? I know it's a 'telescopic sight.' Or are we talking up close and personal – which means blood. How am I supposed to watch Isaac Stalin bleed to death without doing anything? You know, see that I-Thought-You-Loved-Me look on his face and all.*

"You do care, right?" Isaac says. He isn't looking at her eyes. He is looking at the something on her forehead.

"Why would I be here if I didn't?" It's not the most romantic answer. It has occurred to her that Isaac Stalin is looking at the scar above her right eye, the scar he gave her poolside on a winter night.

"—Didn't what?"

"...you know."

"What?"

"—Care about you."

"You sound like it's torture to say it."

This is when Isaac Stalin does something unexpected. He hobbles over to the side of the dirt road and begins to pick some red poppies and blue cliff wildflowers.

Lili has no idea where any of this is going. She has never seen Isaac notice anything on the side of the road.

He hands her the small bouquet. "—Apologies," Isaac says. Isn't quite looking her in the eye, either. "I know I can be a pain in the ass, Li. Maybe I can improve."

What the hell is a person supposed to say? She holds the flowers with both hands, staring down at them.

Isaac Stalin wasn't like her ex. Dr. Norm gave her more than she wanted or required. He'd been Santa Claus if Santa had OCD. That was one reason Lili liked Isaac Stalin. She didn't have to thank him every five minutes.

Oh, God, flowers.

THE OLD MAN SAYS
HE CAN TASTE GOD

Madrid
April 14th, Evening

"YOU MEAN '*SEE* God,' right?"
"I know what I mean, Hillary."

Toward the end of the bullfight, that would be two days ago now, Raymond Mack felt an elephant squat on his chest. *First the damn prostate business, now this*, he thinks. He remembered taking a cell phone call from that whack job Pearlman. Dr. Norm, Lili's ex. But Raymond Mack can't recall what the man said to him.

All he remembers is waking up in a small, immaculate room, hooked to a machine that displayed his vitals and made a steady beeping noise. The room had pale yellow walls and a beige floor.

Hillary Ann Tucker is seated on a plastic chair next to Raymond's bed, her long manicured fingers draping his wrist. A saline drip has been inserted into a vein on the top of his right hand to keep him hydrated. They are at the Hospital Universitario de Madrid.

"What does God taste like?" she says.
"—Wild cherry."
"Maybe somebody gave you a mint."

Her blond hair is in loose strings about her face. She wears no makeup and looks worn. Raymond Mack thinks none of that matters. The girl is a knockout on her worst day.

"This is what you get for hanging out with an old fart,"

the artist says. He likes to say shit like that so she can correct him or playfully chastise him for being *sooooo* wrong.

Hill doesn't reply.

"—*Hey.*"

"I-I thought you were going to die," she whispers. Her eyes water up. When she shuts them, tears run her cheeks. "I should have never let Pearlman call you. Wait 'til I talk to that a-hole. The guy is *always* trouble."

"...Norman, yeah." Ray can't focus his thoughts. "That part I remember."

"He called the apartment," Hill says, wiping her eyes with a wrinkled tissue. "I told him you were at the Bullfight. Every time that man talks to you shit happens. *Every* time. It's unbelievable."

"He means well." Ray hesitates; shakes his head. "— Can't remember a damn thing."

"You scared me, you son-of-a-bitch." Hill says this as nice as can be. She isn't the sort of person who goes all dramatic. Raymond is certain she's basically a very nice girl who has contacts with a lot of very bad people. He knows this like he knows how to draw a straight line. People 101. The basics. Hillary says to him, "You can't die on me, Baby Ray. That's our agreement, remember? Right from the start I said, 'If I fall in love with your old ass, you better not die on me.' And you said, 'Don't worry, Hill, if you fall in love with me, I'll absolutely outlive you.'"

"I thought we were, you know, speaking figuratively."

"I don't speak figuratively about shit like that."

"I can see."

Hillary looks down at her slender fingers spread about his wrist. Her voice is breathy and close to inaudible, "...oh, I know the risks. Old men. When old men leave you, they leave for good."

"I'd stay if I could."

"I know that, too."

When the elephant sat on Raymond Mack's chest, Ray pissed himself. That's how scared he'd gotten. Wet his damn pants, for god-sake. Like those old fools in a nursing home – a drooler, a pooper in your pants , some leftover guy who breaths through his mouth and doesn't know where he is, some old guy who keeps forgetting his name. The elephant made him go over his life, what he had done, what he still wanted to do. Made him think about his daughter Lili.

"You should stop smoking, Baby Ray."

"I don't smoke."

"I smell it on your clothes," Hillary says, very nice, very low-key.

"That's second hand smoke from the bar."

"It's first hand smoke from our patio."

"Okay, you're right," Baby Ray says. He's watching the monitor reading his vitals in green digital neon – his heart rate, his blood pressure, the beep-beep of his life. *Damn, I got to do something.* Then Raymond says, "Who am I kidding? Not you, that's for sure. The drinking, the smoking, its got to go, all of it. I mean this is my life here, *our* lives."

"Lili wants you around, too."

Lili, my sweet girl. This why he hired what's-his-name, Dr. Bolian, or whatever his name was – Dr. Fucking Death. Dying is one thing but dying with scores unsettled is very much another matter.

"—Call your friend," Raymond says to Hill; grips her fingers with his left hand, the one with the wrinkled tissue.

"You're *hurt*ing me." She wiggles herself free. "—And what friend?"

"The guy I gave the 75K to, your doctor friend. You know what friend." He is studying her, trying to get the nuances. *I can never tell what she's thinking.* "The man didn't show, didn't meet with me. If I'm going to die, I want peace of mind. I want to know wrongs will be righted – what's so unusual with that?"

"It was years ago."

"—Not to me. Not to Lili, either."

"Dr. Bolian will do what you paid him to do," Hill says.

Raymond's sure he hears reluctance in her voice. Then his thoughts go to the other matter. What the hell did Norm Pearlman say to him?

GRIGOR BOLIAN GOES TO THERAPY

Lenox Hill Hospital
New York City
September, 1987

BEFORE GRIGOR BECAME a thoracic surgeon, he had explored psychiatry, more specifically, psychoanalysis. Sitting behind the patient appealed to him. Being quiet and listening had a certain charm. Psychiatry was part of his rotation, but he had also been wanting to talk to someone about The Commander. This need began after the Immigration Reform and Control Act of 1986. Mr. Reagan had a way of surprising Grigor with his little islands of compassion.

Who the fuck hears a president talking to him?

"Medical school has its stressors," Dr. Marvin Rosen says. He is a short, thick necked type, reminiscent of a high school weight lifter but with graying hair. All this occurred during Grigor's first session. Rosen is both instructor and therapist and tells him, "You'd be surprised how many students become transiently psychotic."

"Is that what I am – psychotic?" Bolian feels panic rush through his arms and chest, everything hot and electric.

"The emphasis here is on 'transient,' okay?" You can hear the tut-tut, now-now in Rosen's voice. "—Transient, as in 'fleeting,' a momentary drop in life's little bucket."

Like Grigor doesn't know what 'transient" means. "It's *still* psychotic."

101

"Students obsess over labels."

Grigor could have killed Rosen right there. With his hands. Crush his windpipe or yank the arteries from the man's neck with his fucking teeth. What charged his rage was self-absorbed twits – their indifference and condescension. They love to look in the mirror as they talk about you.

Who is this asshole to tell me I'm transiently psychotic, that I am another crazy naïve student obsessing over labels? Really?

Labels?

You know nothing about me, Rosen. I just walked into you're office five, ten minutes ago and you got me fingered out? Is that what you truly think, you grandiose motherfucker? Throw me into some creepy group that will reduce your own anxiety level?

Easy to imagine multiple scenarios.

The rip his cock off and watch him bleed to death scenario. A perennial favorite. The crack his head on the faggy pink marble coffee table and pull out his brain scenario. The hold his head in the toilet bowl until he drowned scenario (never as easy as you see in the movies). There was also the rotate his head and snap his neck scenario, but that would be too quick a death for this bastard.

Anger blooms in Grigor like flames on dry pine and he has to remind himself to –

"You're smiling," Dr. Rosen says.

"I'm enjoying our chat."

"Tell me about the voice you hear," Dr. Rosen says. "This is wonderful, yes? We'll be able to work on a *real* issue."

"—A transient issue."

"So we'll work on it briefly."

Just calm down, Grigor thinks. He leans back in the

tan leather chair, crossing his legs at the knee. *An out of control person is never an effective person. That's what you want the other guy to do.*

He *did* want to understand "The Commander," as he'd begun calling him. "I don't know where to start," Grigor says. "I've never discussed this sort of thing out loud, you know, with others. I'm not the most sharing individual."

"—All the more reason," Dr. Rosen says, writing God-knows-what in a black spiral notebook. Is he afraid he'll forget? Is he writing a Tell-All book? Grigor doesn't like this note-taking crap. Rosen says, "You told me he – The Commander – that he is a former president?"

"—Reagan, yeah. Or has his voice." *Jesus, how do you go about even discussing this.* "I mean I know it's *not* Reagan, okay? I have sense. I'm not one of these loonies with an aluminum foil hat. Guys getting messages from God knows who. It disrupts my life. I find the whole business disturbing."

"Ahh, Reagan. Excellent choice." Dr. Rosen nods and grins but doesn't look up from his note-taking.

Grigor Bolian doesn't like this therapist, this cretin, this bitch boy Jew.

You think a waggy-headed B actor is somehow an "excellent' choice? Grigor doesn't get Marvin Rosen. The *Bonzo Goes to College* guy, an actor, a sportscaster? *Yeah, let's elect that guy.*

"So what does your friend say to you?" Dr. Rosen pauses his note taking and looks up.

This is a bad idea, Grigor is thinking. *Why did I believe I could do therapy? Where's my mind? The Commander is the lease offensive issue I've got.*

No, he didn't have the usual issues of the Worried Well. Resentments toward friends, relatives and coworkers. Erectile Dysfunction. Alcohol, smoking, other drugs and/or weight issues. Anxiety-panic on dates, public

103

speaking, separation, being alone, being with others, being in the dark, on and on. Depression when the world didn't go his way. Gender role inflexibility. Impaired social skills. Obsessive behaviors. Eating or sleeping disorders. Abundant somatic complaints. Stuttering. The endless, mundane list of what happens when you are breathing.

He did not have these concerns.

Shall I tell you about how I murdered my Uncle Revig while he and my mother lay sleeping in the same bed? How I had to lock myself in my room and slip the key under the door so I could avoid killing my mother, too – this fucking whore of a mother. This betrayer of my father. This betrayer of our family?

Shall I tell you what I've done since that time?

THE SCAR

THEY'RE FOLLOWING THE river Arda from Zubiri through smaller villages toward Pamplona. Isaac can't keep track of the names of these places; doesn't want to, really. His scraped right knee still hurts him – a possible infection, who the crap knows – and the blisters on both his heels and the side of his right big toe have slowed him down to limp status.

"Listen, I'm not doing that great myself," Lili says. She is also limping. "A fine pair, aren't we? But, you know, pain is part of the deal."

"No, no." Isaac dismissing that notion with a hand wave. "—*Not* my deal. I made a different deal."

"Think of Jesus walking the via Dolorosa."

"That's one of those 'street cred' walks, believe me."

"I love your sense of humor," Lili says.

This morning she'd lathered their feet with Vaseline. Isaac didn't know how to take it. He remembered looking down at Lili smearing that gunk on his blistered feet and thinking, *What am I supposed do with you? What's a person supposed to say?*

Isaac Stalin and Lili have just hiked from a narrow tunnel cut through the one of the mountains, an opening the size of a coffin. They had to walk single file in the dark to enter the next town. A short walk, though, less than a seventy-five feet. Lili's hand was gripping his shoulder all the way.

"I can barely move," Isaac says. He's been going slow for the last mile. The stone and dirt road is as narrow as the opening in the mountain. On one side of the road the hill goes upward and on the other side the road becomes a drop off. *Easily a hundred feet, probably more,* Isaac thinks. The drop off is filled with mist and tree branches. He says, "If these blisters and my leg don't kill me, falling down into that should do it."

"The first day or two is the worse." Lili is walking behind him. There isn't enough room for them to walk side by side.

"How can you be so cheerful?"

"What's the alternative?"

"Standing still and screaming," Isaac says, sort of joking, sort of not. He hasn't quit looking down at the foggy emptiness of the drop.

A two story chopped stone and white stucco building is now in the distance. It's nestled amid leafless dark trees and tall green shrubs.

He says, "What is that, a hotel? An Inn?"

"—A hotel," Lili says, glancing at her guidebook.

"Food, I hope."

"—Uh-huh, four stars."

Akerreta is the name of the town, one of many on the road to Pamplona. The mountains here are wet and very green from the constant on-again-off-again rain. A mist partly conceals everything and the tree branches show through the mist like a black bony web.

"It kills me, you know," Isaac says.

"Okay. What's killing you *now.*"

He can hear her sarcasm.

First she is nice then she is annoyed. *Typical woman shit,* he thinks. *They're what-you-call-it – flip-floppers, the John Kerry of viginas. How can anybody – any man – count on a woman? This fucking trip is at least teaching me that much – if you don't like how a woman is feeling toward you just hang out another five minutes or so and she'll change her mind.* He's glad she is walking behind him and he doesn't have to look at her.

"You've been very brave," she says.

"—What?"

"I said, 'You're being very —'"

"No, no, I heard you. Thanks." Isaac doesn't turn to look at her. *Okay, so she's maybe different than most women. People can be different. Some glitch in the gene pool, or what-have-you.*

"Sorry this isn't more fun," Lili says.

"No, no, it's okay." Isaac has decided that it is okay after all. *The fact that she even knows it's not okay makes it okay.*

"Maybe salvation and fun don't go together."

"—Yeah, the germs alone." He is thinking about the pilgrim hostels. Bed Bugs on Parade. Oh and another thing: everybody Isaac has met in these hostels loves to talk about how invigorating it is to "overcome" hardships. Their favorite word is "sanctify."

Basically, you want to puke.

This is when he hears his companion scream. He turns and sees her frantically flapping her skinny arms as if she's trying to fly but she is losing her balance and starts falling off the edge of the narrow road and into the mist. Isaac grabs her left arm by the wrist and is pulled to his knees but he doesn't let go. Now he's looking over the edge at her dangling there, suspended only by his hold on her.

"—Shit, shit," Isaac says, mostly to himself. Like what comes next. *What do I do?* He answers his own question, *You lift her ass up. God, you Moron.*

"You can do this, honey," she says. Looks up at him, an anxious smile. "—Take a breath, okay? Go on, a nice big one. I believe in you."

No one had ever called him "honey" before. It left him feeling both creepy and very good. Very, very good, actually. He's looking down at her – Delores Reo, like a movie star from the forties, a B picture queen – this woman, this person who he could save or just open his hand and her let go.

"I'm so glad you're here with me, Isaac." She is saying this as he is secures his grasp about both her wrists.

"—Yeah. Me, too. I'm glad, too." He hears the softness in his voice. The softness is a surprise.

"I knew you'd be there for me, I knew it." She's looking up at him.

That is more than he knew. But, shit, maybe.

As Isaac lifts her, he can see a scar above Lili's right eye. He has seen this scar before, many times, the scar thing isn't a shock. So why is it bothering him now, what's *that* all about?

Lili Mack's face is less than a foot from him as he yanks her onto the stone and dirt road. Isaac collapses beside her – Delores Reo, with her Lauren Bacall voice. The two of them are breathing hard, sharp breaths.

That scar, he is thinking. *I've seen that scar.*

THE WINDMILLS
OF DR. NORM

In bed with Norm and Moana
Kettledrum, Vermont

AT 1:17 AM THE four Ritalin enhanced children are finally asleep thanks to a 2mgs dose of *plot*zepam, whatever the fuck it's called. Dr. Norm is just happy to hear himself think or – in this case – scheme.

"Where are you going again?" His wife, Moana, is in bed and half asleep. She's a big woman in a massive pink rayon nightie. She likes calling herself

"a full-figured gal," what they say in the commercials. Moana will also tell you she has insight into her pizza and soda consumption.

"I ex*plain*ed this," Dr. Norm says, all exasperated.

"Explain it to me again, sweetie."

"—Spain, okay? Jeez-God. A week, maybe less. It's not all that far away. Well, maybe it's far away. But believe me, Moana, this isn't anything shady. Okay? I'm your husband. You should trust your husband."

"I trusted my first one."

"So why not me?" Dr. Norm says.

"Because I trusted my first one."

Mona is a licensed clinical psychologist in the state of Vermont. She understands one trial learning.

"I've had another premonition," Norman Pearlman says, as though it's a shame filled confession. "I love you and the kids, you know that. Who takes you guys to the Dairy Queen? Huh? Who comes with me to catch the Red

Sox – who's that guy? Who buys you and the kiddies dogs and fries? Don't I explain the game and what's up with the players' lives and such?"

"You could've stopped at fries," she says. Since Dr. Norm needed to lose a few pounds himself, he gets the joke.

"There you go. I'm your fry guy. " He taps his chest with a forefinger.

"What was your premonition, exactly?"

"I already said."

"So say it *again*. I mean what the fuck, Norman." Moana is definitely awake now.

"I believe my ex-wife will be stabbed to death."

"I should be so lucky," she says, partly kidding.

Norman ignores her and tries to make his voice very solemn but it comes out cock-eyed and anxious. "The weapon will be an antique surgical blade."

"Oh c'm*on*," Moana says. "It's after one in the morning." Immediately she goes to her question, "How do you know these future events, again? Yes, I know you told me – probably more than once – and I'm aware that my listening skills need improvement, but what was your rationale?"

"I see these events in the stars."

"So science related."

Moonlight is squared off by the two bedroom windows and goes across the shiny cherry wood floor and along the white walls of their bedroom.

"Don't think I don't know sarcasm when I hear it," Dr. Norm says.

"This is about fucking her, isn't it?"

"—Excuse me?"

"Your *ex* – it's about fucking your ex. I see it in my practice constantly. 'Oh I hate you,' they say. 'But I can't live without that pussy, I can't live without that cock.'

You're boarding on being a cliché, you know that? You know what a cliché you are, sweetie?" Moana is now propped up on an elbow, Shamu in repose. "Just don't go getting all innocent on me, Norman. You're like a book I've read a million times."

"I know my predictions aren't science related," he tells her. "—Not any science *I* know. I'm just saying, the success I've had with these predictions, or what*ever* they are, goes beyond chance, beyond anything random."

Well you've saved me and the kids more than once." After admitting that – what's fair is fair – Moana says, "But I know you want to fuck her, okay? Don't think I'm letting that go. I'm not a moron, Norman."

He ignores his wife's comments and goes on with points that give reliability to the mystical. "Remember the downtown bus I keep you and the kids from taking. What happened there – a total wreck, am I right?"

"You *know* what I mean." She is giving him her squinty, I've-Got-Your-Number look. "Why do you keep in contact with her – this Lili Mack person – with the father, too, why do you do that? See, I think it's love. There's something very pathetic about it: wanting to possess the unavailable woman. Right away any decent psychologist would start to think about mother issues."

"I saved your *life*, for gosh-sake – and more than once." Dr. Norm didn't get his wife's resistance to his obvious talent. *Mother issues? Are you kidding? How 'bout me saving you from a car hitting a bus and everything exploding? How bout that one?* "I have a gift," he says. The two of them are in the bed, covered by moonlight. "—An amazing gift. Why can't you acknowledge that? Why can't you support me? Answer that question."

"I'm thinking you want to fuck her."

NIGHT VISITOR

Hospital Universitario de Madrid
April 16th, Evening

GRIGOR BOLIAN THINKS RAYMOND is sleeping but the old man grabs Grigor's wrist just before the doc has a chance to shake him awake.

The old man's eyes blink open. "Who're you, bud?"

"Nice reflexes," Grigor says, a bit of a smile. He'd read about Raymond Mack being shuttled off to the hospital. *One of those holy shit I am mortal moments, no doubt.*

Grigor is standing beside a plastic, red cushioned chair next to the bed. "— Calm down, sport. I'm your employee. You might recall the money you sent to my account a few days ago."

The hospital room is dark except for the neon green lines on the monitor.

"—Dr. Bolian?" Raymond says, something slightly louder than a whisper. "We had a meeting. You're four days late."

"A doctor's life is unpredictable."

"—Not with my money, it isn't."

"Hillary told me you were clever. 'Very Witty,' she said." Grigor studies the old man's face. "You don't look like a witty guy. Tell me a joke. Can you do that? I'm the audience witty guys dream about, I'll laugh at anything."

"And you know Hillary from where?"

"—A mutual friend."

"I can't imagine you having friends."

A new light appears behind Dr. Bolian, something bright and yellow. This is followed by a hard, dime-sized pressure at the back of his head.

The barrel of a pistol, is the doctor's first thought.

"Turn to me, please. But slow." A woman's voice. Her arms are outstretched. A two-toned Pico .380 semi-automatic is pointed at Grigor's face. Her left hand is under her right to keep the weapon steady. The yellow light is coming from the small bathroom behind her. The woman says, "You don't come here any time you want, Bolian. Visiting hours apply."

"I'm a physician."

"I don't care if you're Dr. Zhivago," she says. Her eyes don't leave him. "You'll see Mr. Mack when I see Mr. Mack. That means *only* when I'm here."

As Grigor adjusts to the light, "—Is that you, Hillary?" *Still hot after all these years.* "How you doing, darlin'?"

"Don't 'darling' me."

"I'm trying to have a meeting." Dr. Bolian's hands are raised and his smile is wide and frozen. "Let me add, a meeting set up by *your* significant other. Not by me, okay? *I'm* paying respects. I'm here by invite. Glad you've showed, though. Old friends and all."

"We're not friends."

Grigor ignores her comment. "Let me thank you for the recommendation." He nods to Raymond. Then he says, "May I put my hands down? I have every intention of being a good fellow, believe me."

"Is your money in the bank?" She doesn't lower the Pico .380. The doctor isn't answering her. She says, "You *have* the money?"

"—Yes."

"Then go do your job."

Now his palm is to his heart. You wound me," Grigor says. And looking at the old man. "They all hurt you eventually, don't they? Our pretty girls, our dears. We think we know them, but we know is what they want us to know. The rest is a fantasy, our imagination, our slight-of-hand, our tricks with mirrors. It's sad all around."

What would our mutual friend say? he thinks. *Oh I know you remember. How chummy we were on the phone, how flirtatious. What would our mutual friend say, if that friend saw you aiming a firearm at your devoted Grigor? What would they all say, our nervous little group?*

Hillary is fixing a silencer on the Pico .380.

"I'll put you down and throw you out the window," Hill says, no emotion. She could've been telling him who won yesterday's ballgame or what she had for lunch. "I don't much care about you, or Raymond's brilliant revenge fantasy. Part of me knows this is a mistake – killing some middle-aged douchebag for something he did when he was a kid. This shit is more for Raymond's ego than his daughter."

"Hear that, Raymond?" Dr. Bolian gives a glance at the old man whose eyes are closed, his breathing easy. *So not exciting enough for you?*

"What's the old man gonna do?" Hillary says, aiming the pistol at Bolian's forehead, the silencer attached and ready. "Beat me up? He's amazed I want to fuck him. And I do, you know. I like fucking Raymond."

"—T.M.I." Immediately Grigor presses his palms against his hear, grinning, feigning embarrassment.

"The past is the past, isn't that what people say?" Hillary's thin arms are still stretched outward and stiff. She is circling him, the Pico aimed at his head. "Enemies become friends. Everything can change – except dying and assholes." After making a full, tight circle, Hill hesitates; stares at him before saying, "Those who've hurt us can show remorse. That happens every day. Surprises abound. I don't know what goes on between two people. Do you? Who's to say if Lili's life could have been better if she'd gone to this school or gotten that job. If dreams weren't stolen. You have to wait for the end of a life to add it up, to figure the wins and the losses."

"Why don't you put that gun down."

"I like you nervous."

"Silencers are bullshit, dear," Grigor says. She is right. He can hear the anxiety in his voice. "You know their bullshit, right? Something for the movies. Guns always make noise."

"Nothing wrong with a little noise."

That's it, that's Dr. Bolian's limit. He can feel the last of his patience fold in on itself. In one motion he pulls the pistol from Hillary as the side of his foot hits the back of her leg. She falls backward and hits the ground hard enough to knock the breath from her. His knee is on Hill's chest, the pistol at her forehead.

"Now I'm all annoyed," Grigor whispers. He's looking over at the hospital bed. Raymond is asleep, the vital signs on the monitor beside the bed beeps evenly. Neon green lines show his heartbeat rising and falling with a steady rhythm. Grigor whispers to Hillary, "Now anything can happen, you understand? Yes, I have your money. Good luck getting it back. Now here's what you've done, you and your attitude. I take a little out of the daughter for this insult, for this inconvenience."

"Get off of me."

"When I'm ready."

THE SCAR
PART 2

The mountain town of Akerreta
April 16th

THAT SCAR, HE'S thinking, *I know that scar.*
Isaac Stalin has just saved Lili from falling into a very deep ravine, he's not sure how deep. The drop is filled with mist and the dark branches of trees. She'd slipped and fallen from the edge of the narrow mountain road on the way to Akerreta.

The two are on their backs, breathing hard and trying to get calm.

"What's your real name?" Isaac says this between short, audible breaths.

"—My what?"

"—You're real *name.*" Isaac Stalin isn't sure what he means by that. It's more of a feeling, an unknown thing close enough to grab. He does another audible inhale. "What can I tell you? I always thought you stole your name from one of those old Huston films,

The Maltese Falcon, or whatever. 'Delores Reo' – it's Hollywood for 'mystery name.'

Who calls themselves that?"

Lili ignores his question. "Thanks for catching me, Isaac." A very sweet voice, he believes, very endearing. "I would've probably died. God that's *so* creepy to think about. Dying is something that happens to everybody else." Lili is still trying to relax her breathing. "I mean I know I'm *going* to die one day, but 'one day' is always *out* there, you know, over the next mountain – until you get too close." She shuts her eyes; takes another inhale and says, "... then it's everywhere, all at once. I-I owe you big time."

Isaac rolls to his side, looking down at her face. He examines the scar above her right eye. Traces it with his index finger. Lili winces at his touch.

"Does it hurt?" he says.

"I'm self-conscious, that's all."

"Hey I think you're lovely."

That didn't come out right, too reassuring, too whatever, condescending. Compliments are such suspicious things. Isaac didn't mean it that way. And she didn't need his sympathy – Lili would be forever lovely. People like looking at Lili. He could walk down the street with her and see it. He's not a blind man, for God-sake. She doesn't need reassurance. Isaac can't figure why he'd said what he'd said. Every once in awhile shit just comes out.

"You don't have to tell me that." Lili says.

"Oh you're right, you're absolutely right." He can tell she's embarrassed. "What I *mean* is, don't worry about the scar. Okay? I always wanted you to know that. People worry too much about stuff that nobody notices – or if they do, they find charming. The scar doesn't matter. It keeps you from becoming a – what-you-call it – a mannequin. A Miss Perfect. It let's us average guys feel comfortable around you."

"That's very sweet."

"Fuck 'sweet.' It's true."

He'd never been good with women. Or people in general, when he thought about it. He had no male buddies or friends, you know, guy *pals – or whatever you're supposed to call these assholes.* Bro-loves. But women were puzzles without clues. Women had this timeless uncertainty. They'd hide themselves in makeup and pretty smells. They'd let you imagine them. *Shape me as you want me*, their hidden self would say. *Build us on your desire, your sniff, your touch, the place known for its throb and stretch.*

Thank God for the Pair-Up dating site. *As banal as it is*, he thinks. *That was an online miracle.* He still doesn't get why a person like Lili Mack finds him desirable or "interesting" or who-knows-what – *compatible.* Such a woman's word – *compatible.* Men don't *ever* use that word. Men just want to know if a woman can come.

Cum.

Can you cum? When are you cumming? Do you like it when we cum together? The three basic questions of good dating. It's like the three major food groups.

Isaac never had been that sort of man. He didn't know what sort of man he was, hadn't given the subject consideration. But he knew everything between them had shifted. He'd reached out and caught her wrist and pulled her up without giving it a thought. Isn't that what people do? *No one tells you what saving somebody does to you, how it's going to make you feel.* Maybe it's different for everyone. He feels ... well ... protective. Isn't that it?

Like you're responsible for the person you save – what the Indians always tell you – and not responsible in a bad way. It's not like my responsibility to take out the garbage or do the grocery shopping. You actually want to watch over this individual, you want to take care of her.

To... shit, what can I say? To love her.

Lili lightly presses her fingertips to his cheek. "You look *so* worried. I'm okay.

We're okay, I swear. We're better than okay. That's what this trip is all about, getting through things together."

"I never saved anybody."

"You made big deposits in my Bank 'O Love, Isaac Boy."

"It's amazing, isn't it?"

Lili puts her palm behind his neck and guides him down to her and kisses him.

"It's very amazing," she whispers.

"...Jesus, I feel stupid." Then Isaac sees the expression on her face, how it alters, her whole face has a new set of feelings. He says, "I don't mean anything negative, I really don't. What's wrong baby?"

"I dunno." Lili shuts her eyes. "Yes, I do. We have to talk."

THE EFFECTS OF
PREMONITION

Madrid-Barajas Airport
Mid-morning

THE INSIDE OF the Madrid-Barajas Airport resembles
the chest cavity of an enormous bug. There's a billowy
yellow ceiling, and the yellow floor to ceiling beams are
slanted.

— *Like ribs*, Dr. Norm trying to pull it all together, let
a bit of sense into it. *The beams are the ribs of the bug.*
They even curve a little like ribs.

He feels positively Kafkaesque.

Or psychotic, or what he thinks about when he thinks
about psychosis – *it's all very exhilarating.*

Now he pauses in front of a full length mirror next to a
concession stand that sells newspapers, fruits and coffee.
He is looking in the mirror to make sure he hasn't grown
antennas.

"Se sientes enfermo, senor?" A woman is behind him.

When Dr. Norm turns from the mirror, he sees a nun,
perhaps someone from the Convento de Corpus Cristi, the
only convent he's read about in the travel guide. She's very
young with lovely tan skin and rimless glasses, a pretty girl
who is wearing white robes and a white covering that
frames her face. He's figuring a hospital nun, maybe a
nurse, whatever.

"My Spanish isn't the best," he says.

"Are you sick?" She has a thick accent, that lispy thing
Spaniards do when they're speaking English. The nun

introduces herself as Sister Claudia. Then she says, "Do you need the hospital?"

"Do I need what?" When he quits scrutinizing his reflection and thinks about her words, he says, "No, no, but you're *very* kind. Thank you."

Dr. Norm wants to tell Sister Claudia how they are in the stomach of a big yellow bug but he still has enough sense to know a shaky conversation choice.

"—Jet lag," Norm says.

The sister doesn't look convinced. She buys two coffees from the old man at the concession stand and hands Norm one and nods toward the small metal and bright plastic tables near the newspapers and magazines.

"Sit with me," she says and pats the chair next to her. "We can have a coffee and talk about the day. I just saw a young man off who is going home to have hand surgery. He's German and doesn't trust our Spanish doctors. What can a person do? We all have our prejudices, yes?"

"Your English is wonderful." Dr. Norm sees her look down at her Styrofoam coffee cup, maybe embarrassed. "Have I said something wrong?"

Sister Claudia shakes her head but continues to look at her cup. "I apologize, senor. I'm no good at compliments, even innocent ones."

"If only my students were like you," Dr. Norm says. He's already smiling, he can't help himself. "The ones who deserve compliments are always too embarrassed to take them."

His laugh is forced but the she doesn't join him. Maybe it's not so much a laugh as what his wife calls, *"Your phony-baloney good time."* Norman is trying to relax her, that's all. *What's so wrong with that?* he'd like to know.

Sunshine is going through a glass wall and the light reflects off the polished floor and the yellow ceiling and surrounds them in light. What with the nun's white robes, Norm can barely see her.

Claudia has taken a pocket-sized spiral notebook and ballpoint pen from an invisible pocket in the drape of her habit.

"This is such good advice." She has begun to write, a tiny, exact script. "I want to remember. It's so obvious. I must work on my humility. I can't tell you how often the sisters have urged me toward that simple truth, but I was too prideful. I have always been a bit of a show off, I'm afraid."

"No, that's not what I meant," he's thinking. He doesn't know how she came up with that one. *"Really. Life is way too serious to take the little things so seriously."*

Dr. Norm wants to tell her about his special gift, his premonitions given to him by the stars, by the universe itself, but he doesn't know if the news would calm her or make the whole matter worse.

"Pay attention to the sky," he'd like to say to her. *"That's all you have to do; that's all anyone has to do – pay attention. The stars have been here before us and they will be here after us. They are the wise gentlemen and ladies of the universe. They are God's well intended servants, but they have stolen secrets they wish to share. 'The sky is forever filled with the musings of God,' they'll tell you, 'God's thoughts whisper through the nebulas, his breath gives flame to new stars.'* What would his dear nun do with that info? Would she write it down? Would she throw away her pen?

Dr. Norm wants to tell the sister that he has come to this place to save the lives of his ex-wife and her new boyfriend, that his first premonition had been incorrect. At first he thought only the boyfriend would be harmed.

Okay, not harmed – killed.

Then last night a new musing appeared in the sky. The

heavens had added Lili Mack to its list. Who or what would kill them, Dr. Norm didn't know. But he did know the "how" of it. The antique surgical knife seen at the start hadn't changed. He'd even looked up the image of the knife online, a Jacob J. Teufel, *circa* 1870s.

NIGHT VISITOR
PART 2

Hospital Universitario de Madrid
April 16th, Evening

HILLARY ANN TUCKER doesn't want some psycho shooting her with her own gun.

Get off me, you discussing creep.

She's laying on the polished, moonlit floor of Raymond Mack's hospital room.

The old man is in the bed and looks asleep or drugged or both. Grigor has straddled her waist, pressing the barrel the Pico .380's silencer against Hill's forehead. The room is deeply shadowed except for the green digitalized lines and numbers on dear Baby-Ray's monitor and a slice of light behind them coming from the partially opened bathroom door.

"Now you're getting an extra one for free." Grigor means Hill's pistol wagging behavior hasn't pleased him and he's decided to kill Lili, too.

"Hurt her and I'll find you."

"Whoa." He grins. "So rough and tough."

"—Little bitch boy," she whispers.

The flat of his hand goes across Hill's face. He pulls her head back and shoves the Pico under her chin.

"Want to see if the silencer works?" he says.

"Didn't you tell me silencers are bullshit?"

"I lied."

Hillary is faster than she imagines. She grabs Grigor's wrist and yanks the Pico .380 away from her forehead and to the left. Right away the thing fires. Grigor has a startled look and drops the pistol. Maybe he thinks the thing fired itself.

Hell, who knows what a guy like that thinks.

Grigor's right, though, even with a silencer the sound is loud enough to leave the inside of Hill's ears throbbing. For a second or two the world goes silent.

Now she thrusts both hands against the man's chest and catches him off balance. Grigor falls to the left; Hillary rolls to the right. She sees the pistol a yard or so away and goes after it on all fours, Grigor not that far behind her. Hill collapses on top of the Pico.

The door has opened. Yellow light from the hallway goes across the floor and flashes on the windows. This is also when Raymond Mack wakes and looks about the room.

"What was that?" the RN says. She's at the doorway – Emily Rodriguez. Hill has talked to the woman a couple of times – conversations about kids and bad husbands, mostly – and Hill likes her. Emily is scanning the room in a fearful way. She's a short woman with thick legs and arms. The RN says, "What are you people doing? What's that noise?"

"We're asking the same question," Grigor says, calm, smiling. He stands and brushes his tan chinos with the flat of his hand. "Scared the hell out of us, as you can see."

"—Hillary?" The nurse has taken a hesitant step into the room. Hill is still face down on the floor. "What're you doing there. Are you hurt?"

"—No, no. fine."

"You don't look fine."

"I got scared, that's all." Hillary's trying to figure out what to do with the pistol that's pressed between the floor and her stomach. "I thought somebody was shooting at us. People are crazy nowadays. Scared the crap out of me,

Emily. The sound was so loud and close. Probably the backfire of a car, I dunno."

"That's what I think," Grigor says.

Raymond raises his head, about to speak. Then all expression leaves him. His eyes blink and close. His head sinks into the pillow.

The RN hasn't stopped glancing about the room. *Semi-frantic eyes*, Hill thinks. Emily is inspecting things but without taking anymore steps into the room. One step is more than enough. But she's doing her inventory, looking for hints, Raymond Mack's IV, Raymond's monitor, the windows – probably for bullet holes –the open bathroom door, signs of crazy shit. The RN appears stuck in place. Maybe she wants to move but can't move. Maybe she wants to make accusations but doesn't have enough evidence to work the room. Hill thinks the nurse is feeling danger and duty in equal amounts.

"Everything is okay," Hillary says, but not getting up from the floor. Her hand has definitely found the Pico .380 under her, and Hill's trigger finger is definitely on the trigger. "I just want to stay here for a second or two. You know, catch my breath."

"Rattled our nerves for sure," Grigor says.

Both Hill and the doc smile at Emily. They're staring at her but keep quiet. The RN turns and leaves; saying, "If this happens again..." Her words end there, perhaps not knowing what she'd do if she heard the same noise again.

When Rodriguez is gone, Hill quickly rolls onto her back, aiming the Pico at Grigor Bolian's chest.

NIGHT OF THE LIVING TRUTH

Pamplona
April 20ᵗʰ, Present

DELORES REO IS definitely that girl, that Lili Somebody. *'Mack,' wasn't that her last name?* Isaac Stalin is almost a hundred percent sure, maybe ninety-five percent. In that ballpark.

Lili Mack. Leelee.

He's laying on one of the double decker beds above Lili-Delores-Whoever at the St. James Hostel in Pamplona. The room has four double-deckers, eight people sleeping, eight people breathing out various noises. The mattresses are very hard and narrow and reek with other people's sweat. Moonlight is coming through the windows and across the wood floor in wide silver strips. Isaac thinks about what he had to do to get his cello scholarship at the Casaux in Madrid, so many years ago now, what he did to Lili Mack. It's all pouring into him, all the little factoids he'd tucked away from himself.

... people and animals – hell, life itself, no question about it, life itself – will do anything to survive – just about anything, okay – and more than survive, people will do anything to FLOURISH – people and animals. And isn't that the key word – flourish? Isn't that the key to absolutely everything? It's biological, okay? No, it's more than that, it's Darwinian. Yes, there you go, I said it, or thought it, that evil name, that ugliest of ugly utterances – Darwinian.

Live with it, bitches.

It's the Ying and fucking Yang of your life.

So why the guilt? That's how it felt. It felt precisely like guilt, and he knew he had it and didn't know how to lose it.

We fight for what we want, don't we?

Nobody hands you shit and nobody gives you a free ride, a free anything. 'Free' is another word for 'chump.' Everybody but the chumps know that. Strings are the name of the game. Strings are tied to all things: 'I will do whatever for you but you've got to do for me.' And we're not talking survival – ants survive, bacteria survive. What we're talking is FLOURISHING. We're talking I kick your ass before you kick mine. There's no room at the top for kum-ba-yah.

"Are you asleep?"

Isaac hears Lili Mack, a whisper from the bunk under him.

"I feel bugs," he whispers back.

"It's part of the ambiance."

"You're name isn't Delores, am I right?" He just comes right out with it.

"—A regular Sherlock," she says. Doesn't miss a beat.

"When were you gonna tell me? Or were you?"

"I thought about it after you saved my life." Lili's voice is quiet, breathy. "But I wasn't sure how you'd take it. Remember that Jack Nicholson movie? You know where Jack says to Tom Cruise, 'You can't handle the truth.' God I *loved* that movie."

Isaac feels a hot flush go across his skin. "—What a fool I am." He says this out loud but more to himself than to her. Then he says, "What's this trip about, Lili? That's your names, isn't it? Lili Mack?"

"—Yes."

"What's this trip about, Lili Mack?"

"You're Sherlock. Figure it out."

"Getting even, the Casaux thing?" Isaac hears his voice go shaky. He hears that shakiness again when he says, "So what's the real story? Are we a sham here, or what? You have no feelings for me?"

"—Not at first, I didn't," Lili says, all matter-of-fact. "My father got me worked up. The injustice of it, how it ruined my life, or was supposed to ruin it. But when I think about it, it didn't ruin my life. It didn't ruin anything. Yeah, I was hurt, particularly at first. Oh poor me, oh how awful. I was so very young, you know. I'd thought, who makes love to somebody and never calls them?' Only later I realized that almost everybody did that."

"Jesus, I *am* a fool." Isaac hears a *shhh* from two or three people in the shadows. His voice becomes a whisper again, "The sexy talk on the phone, what was that, exactly?

Bullshit, right?"

"Why do things have to be either-or? Must a person be madly in love to have phone sex? It's *phone* sex."

Shhhh. Another pilgrim in the darkness.

"—And now?" Isaac whispers.

"—'And now' what?"

"Do you—" he hesitates, unsure how to express his thought without giving away too much of himself to potential wounds. "—Do you ... *you* know ... love me, or *care* for me, whatever you want to call it."

Oh how intelligent does that sound? he thinks. *Balls are not Chanukah presents. Stop giving them away.*

"...yes." Lil says.

"—Yes, what? Yes, I care. Yes, I don't care."

"Yes, I *do* care." This is followed by, "I dunno, maybe *more* than care."

"—Seriously?"

"Don't push it, Sherlock."

"Oh, no, no. De*fi*nitely. No pushing."

Shhhh.

"Hey. Fuck you, kid." Isaac says this to the nameless asshole in the dark room who gave him the shush.

"—Fuck you back," the asshole says.

"I'm sure God loves *that*."

No reply.

Now others in the darkness either mutter *Shhhh* or laugh.

"—Listen to me, Lili says.

"...w-what?" Already prepared for Lili-Delores to either clarify her good feelings for him or take away everything. His bet is on taking away everything.

"Are you listening?"

"—Just go ahead, for god-sake." Ready for the worse.

But neither of those two things happen. She doesn't give, she doesn't take away. This isn't where Lili Mack is going. Instead, she says, "—That's not the most important thing, okay? Maybe I should say, it's not the most *immediate* thing."

"—I-I don't understand."

"Try to focus," she whispers. "Daddy's hired somebody."

"What'd you mean? Like an employee?"

WHY BABY-RAY'S
HEART ATTACKED HIM

Kettledrum College Observatory
April 12th, Evening

RAYMOND MACK'S CELL is ringing, Dr. Norm can hear it.

C'mon, c'mon.

Just getting the cell was a trauma. He'd called Mack's home in Glenside, Pennsylvania and the recorded message said Ray was out of the country. Norm knew what that meant, so he called the guy's apartment in Spain.

It's 8:10 AM in Kettledrum and 2:10 PM in Santiago.

Then Dr. Norm has to go through all of this:

"—Oh you," Hillary says, already annoyed.

"So still with the old man?"

"So still no social skills, *Nor*man?" She found his name amusing. *Nor*man.

"Let me talk to Ray."

"He's at the bullfight."

"—His cell, please."

"What's this about?" Hill says, her protective mode. "I'm not having you get all crazy on him. That's what you do, you know."

"I'm aware you think that." He's sitting on a stool in front of a twelve inch Zeiss refracting telescope, huffing on his pipe. The "twelve inches" is the diameter of the glass lens in the front of a sixteen foot long telescope tube. The room is chilled and the coffee is cold and Norm would much rather be in bed. He doesn't know why Hillary would

133

think he likes calling his former father-in-law and delivering what will surely be viewed by Hill as bizarre news.

"What's this about?" Hill says.

"It's personal, between me and Raymond."

"Is this another one of your psychotic predictions? What's it this time? Did'ya look into your telescope and see Jesus, something like that?"

"—Just give me his cell, please."

"I'm not going to let you screw with Ray's mind."

"Raymond's sixty-two years old," Dr. Norm says. He can hear the irritation in his voice. "He's only old because *you're* young. I'm trying to be a gentleman here, okay? Why don't we let him make his own decisions – unless Alzheimer's has taken over his brain. Is that your story, Hill? Is Ray crapping in his pants and drooling. You gonna go with that?"

"Go away, *Norman*."

Not today, lady. Norm Pearlman stays quiet.

"God, all right, *fine*," Hill says, a weary tone. Probably just wanting to get rid of him, that's what Norm thinks. She says, "—Be respectful."

"I'm always respectful."

That's how Dr. Norm finally got the number. Now he's pacing back and forth

in the observatory. Raymond Mack's cell is still ringing.

Norm switches ears.

C'mon, c'mon.

"How did you get this cell?" Ray says, his first words.

"—From Hillary."

"What did you do to her?" Ray's second words. "I got to live with this woman, you prick. Understand what I'm saying? You think it's easy? You think the only thing I have to do is take Cialis and the world's rosy? Are you that naïve?'

"I believe Lili's life is in danger," Dr. Norm says. He's listening to the drama in his voice and tries to calm himself, or least to sound reasonable. "I saw it this morning,

Raymond. Right here at the observatory. I called you first thing, of course. Look, I realize you and I have differences, that me marrying your daughter wasn't one of your shiniest moments. I get that. If I'm anything, I'm insightful. But I think you can agree that my interest in your daughter is, you know, sincere. Can we agree on that, Ray?"

No reply.

"—Ray?"

No reply.

"I'll take your silence as a 'yes.' I'll take it as a man who's contemplating a myriad of scenarios. Am I right, Ray? Is that what you're doing? You got that 'myriad of scenarios' going on? Look, it's my nature to protect those that I love, Ray, that I will *al*ways love. So I'm going with a 'yes' from you, okay? I'm going to guess you're thinking, 'I may believe Norm is one of those asshole, jewy academics – a Mr. Chips always at loose ends type of guy – but you also know I've got some info you'd be out of your mind to ignore. I'm right, aren't I? Isn't that what you're thinking?"

"What's wrong with you, Norm?"

"Don't pretend you aren't interested, Raymond. Okay? I'm simply being honest right now. I'm not the fool you think I am. All right, yes, yes, I know, I'm aware. 'Why is this insane fool continuing to call me?' you're thinking. Listen, Ray, you and I might not always agree with each other. And I accept that, I know that. Believe me, this boy knows *you* by heart. So here it comes, Ray, hot off the presses. And you should keep in mind my very good track record with the premonition thing. Didn't I predict you'd meet Hillary? Didn't I tell you to get your prostate checked? Remember those predictions?

Pretty good batting record, don't you think?"

"Fine. Get to your point."

"That's what I like about you, Ray. You're a cut-to-the-chase type of individual.

The guy you hired to kill this Isaac Somebody is going to kill your daughter, too. Okay, wait a minute, before you say anything – I'm not sure why. I mean I wish I had answers for everything but I don't, I just don't. Shoot me, right? No, don't shoot me. That's what you call a 'figure of speech.' But you know what I mean." Then Norman Pearlman whispers into the phone, "I'm telling you the stars have shifted. A very dramatic shift. Are you listening to me? You're plan is about to explode in your face, Ray. It's not just the Stalin boy, anymore. It's your daughter, too."

Silence.

"—Ray?"

No answer.

"Are you all right, Ray?"

Dr. Norm hears the phone drop.

THE PROBLEM WITH FATHERS

Pamplona
April 21th, Present

"TO KILL ME? Are you kidding?" Isaac can't believe it.

"I'm his little girl," Lili whispers. "You know daddies."

"—But to *kill* me?"

What can a person say? she thinks. *Dealing with my father is like trying to walk in a hurricane.* Lili knows that the plan told to her was about scaring Isaac Stalin and not about murdering him. *But of course it's about murdering him. How naïve am I, for god-sake?* Now she confesses to Isaac, "I don't know if the guy daddy |hired is just for show – you know, to shake our cages – or if it's ... more."

"Who *does* that?"

"I'm being honest here."

"—A little late in the day, yes?"

A bit of pink cuts the dark sky. Others at the St. James Hostel are sleeping, breathy little sounds. Isaac and Lili Mack are doing their best not to wake them. They are sitting on the lower bunk bed, Lili's bed, their backs pressed to the shadowy wall.

"Daddy blames you for my life not being perfect," she says; wants the idea to sound humorous. Gives him a half-hearted grin.

Oh stupid daddy.

Such a big silly.

Isaac isn't buying the humor angle. He looks shaken.

137

And who can blame him?

An assassin sneaking about the Way of St. James has a particular creepy sort of irony, salvation being tough enough without spicing the pot. Lili sees what she has caused, how

Isaac's arms hug his legs to his chest, the ever-so-slight rocking motion of his body, but she wants no surprises between them.

They must be vigilant together.

If a guy saves your life, you at least have to tell him what's going on.

"My father thinks he's going to die – his prostate cancer," Lili says. She wants to tell him what she knows. "The doctor and everybody else is trying to convince him that the cancer will outlive us all, but he's not buying it. He's thinking about his legacy, what he'll leave behind, how people will remember him. And I'm part of that. Daddy's going to right my wrongs or die trying. It'd be sweet if it wasn't so weird. He's like a president who's obsessing about his library, his place in the history books. You know, 'How can I make myself and every person who's had anything to do with me look good, particularly family members.' I'm not sure how else to put it."

"So he's tying up loose ends?"

"—For better or worse."

"And he blames *me*?" Isaac can't believe it.

"Who's he gonna blame?" Lili Mack is attempting to keep her voice calm and quiet. She doesn't want to crank Isaac's angry feelings another decibel or wake any of the sleeping pilgrims in the hostel. She says, "What can I tell you? He's an old guy. He wants to leave his daughter a perfect world before he dies."

"I was a kid. Doesn't he know that?"

Lili can't believe this guy's brain. "You pushing me into the family pool that night changed my life for the worse," she says. "I think you know that. I *know* you know that. Severe damage to my hearing, remember?" Her anger is controlled but obvious. She gives Isaac a sideways glance and he looks away. "Sorry, but you should give my father that much. He *deserves* that much. You did a cruel and stupid thing."

"My dad was giving me pep talks. 'You got to go after what you want, you got to take it. You don't ask permission.' That's what I was getting. Crush and destroy, my father's motto." He is silent for a moment; then, "...I was fifteen."

"So was King Tut."

His expression spirals into blank, dead eyes.

"C'mon now," Lili whispers. She gently takes his chin between her thumb and forefinger and turns his face toward her. "You were old enough. I could've won that scholarship, gone to the Casaux. I could've whipped your ass, Isaac, there was a good chance. Could've whipped you bad – you *know* that, don't you? I know you do, or you wouldn't have done your 'Push the Girl into the Pool' shit."

"He going to kill me," Isaac says, more to himself.

She puts her finger to his lips. "—Hey, hey," Lili says, her voice still soft, still quiet. "That's not happening. Okay? You saved my life. Now I save yours. You and me, Isaac, all right? Is that okay with you? I'm forty-two years old. I love my father but I'm nobody's little girl. I haven't been a little girl for a very long time. And maybe I should say for the record, you're no fifteen year old kid, either. You're right, those days are behind us."

"Where's this guy? Who is he?"

"Shit if I know, I wish I did."

"—Great."

"You know what I think?" Lili didn't wait for him to answer. "Our lives were being run by two ego-maniacs, that's what I think. Our so-called 'fathers.' Two 'take no prisoners' types, if you ask me."

"What am I suppose to do now?"

"We grow up and figure it out."

"Right. What does that even mean?" Isaac is watching the early morning sunlight go through the windows of the hostel and across the scared wood floor. The pink in the sky is gone. "I say we go to whatever airport is the closest and get the fuck on a plane."

"The guy my father hired, you don't think he'll follow us?"

"—Do you?" Now Isaac's looking very worried.

"I'm guessing guys like that don't care where they kill you," Lili says. "A job's a job, and money is money."

PILGRIM OF THE SKIES

Cathedral of Santiago de Compostela
April 21ⁿᵈ, Mid-day

GARGOYLES DRAIN AWAY the rain and guard the Cathedral of Santiago de Compostela from demons. So Gothic, this temple, so prepared for the dark and fiery assault – each gargoyle is poised, protective. The Compostela with its gray spires has a history of deep spiritual power and loves to taunt the unsuspecting demon. *"C'mon, big boy, come and get me,"* that's how Norman Pearlman imagines it. *"Give me whatever hell you got."*

"You that doctor?" the woman says. She is examining his face as if the "doctor" part of him could be seen in an expression, maybe the color of the eyes, the line of the chin. Dr. Norm guesses she's mid-seventies. Her face is narrow and smooth, such a serene face, ageless. It's the back of her hands that gives her away, the bulge of the veins, the pancake brown spots. She's a very pretty woman, though, especially the hair tied in a bun, black hair with white streaks. *Dramatic hair*, he thinks. *The sort you'd see in a 60s Fellini film.* Then the woman says, "— You Muslim or a Jew?" She says this matter-of-factly.

"—A Jew," Dr. Norm says.

He has come to the cathedral to get information about Lili and Stalin, where they might be, where he should begin his search. But Hillary didn't want to meet with him; *ordered* him to say away from Raymond, too. "Go to the church," another order. "I'll send someone."

"Well you're a very worried Jew," the older woman says.

"You can see that?"

"Churches aren't easy for you."

"—Including my own." Norman Pearlman likes her. She has concern for him, he hears it in her voice. He sees it in her enormous dark eyes and how emotive lines appear and shadow her face. The physicist introduces himself as "Dr. Norm." She tells him her name is Fiorella. Dr. Norm says, "What should I do if I've become fretful about a dear friend's future?"

"I would pray," Fiorella says. Her English is good and what accent she has doesn't get in the way. "Is this a desperate time?"

"More than I want to admit."

Dr. Norm is thinking about the folded piece of white paper in the pocket of his Levi 501s. The folded paper has the name and address of a small arms dealer in Santiago – many brands, Smith and Wesson, Beretta, Glock, Ruger, Taurus, Sako, Puma, etcetera, etcetera. Guns and ammo. He has been taking firearm lessons from one of his graduate students, Lydia Pepper, a blond girl with pulled back hair and short, muscular legs and a faint spray of pox marks on her left cheek from adolescence. Dr. Norm has been to her family's farm in Kettledrum on five different occasions for a hour or two of instruction and target practice. Lydia's father, Desmond, has five pistols, four rifles, one Mossberg 12 gauge, and some ninja oriented weapons like shuriken, nunchakus, kakute rings, and so on.

Lydia's advice is, why carry internationally when you can buy locally?

Fiorella is saying, "...you should also light a candle – for Saint Jude. He's our saint of desperate cases."

The inside of the Compostela reminds Dr. Norm of an immense marble cave.

Tall, gray archways loom on both sides of the long isle.

These arches align themselves with the wood pews. Suspended from the high ceiling are crystal chandeliers that burn yellow and lead to an alter in the distance.

"—Dr. Norm?" Fiorella says, as if the name has reminded her of something. "Are you Norman Pearlman?"

Norm hadn't mentioned his last name. He is on his guard. "I don't see how that's your business, do you?"

"Please, I'm only the messenger," she says, patting his arm. The pats are soft and quick and hardly felt. "Don't start your worrying, doctor. I see the worry coming back to those eyes. Your eyes get dark and you empty them."

"All right. From whom?" Norm wants to have "friendly" eyes but he doesn't know where to begin.

"—Miss Hillary," Fiorella says and puts an index finger to her very red lips. "Wait a minute, I'm trying to recall." Her face brightens. "Pam*plon*a. They are in Pamplona, or they were last night – the ones you're looking for, your ex-wife and her friend."

"Her name is Lili."

"—Lili, yes. And a companion."

Norm Pearlman has read up on The Way of St. James, the hike his ex is taking with her new friend, Isaac Somebody. Shithead. Isaac Shithead. Now Norman knows where to begin – Pamplona.

Thank you, Hillary, he thinks. *At least I have a city, a place to start. First the gun dealer then Pamplona.*

"Well a prayer wouldn't hurt," Dr. Norm says, going back to Fiorella and their talk about St. Jude. "My ex may very well be in a life and death situation. 'Desperate,' yes. That's it, exactly." He's grateful that Fiorella has presented herself, and he feels the muscles in his shoulders and neck start to relax. He hesitates before saying, "I-I don't know what to do with the candles."

"I'll help," she says. "Candles are how we seeks favors, how we get the saint's attention. It's like leaving a voice mail."

"I *love* that." Pearlman is nodding and grinning, it's a truly appealing notion. So a saint is like your attorney, the guy who pleads your case, the guy who knows the legalese, the "God Language," how getting things done works. Dr. Norm says, "I like the whole 'go-between' idea. Jews pray, too, you know? I'm sure you know. But nothing fancy. We've got no go between, no 'in,' with God. You pray your best prayer and hope it's a light traffic day. I mean all of us hope *some*body's home, but who knows."

"Let me show you how to do the candles."

"You're very kind," Dr. Norm says.

Fiorella loops her arm about his, holding tight. They walk down the marble isle carpeted to the front of the cathedral and the candle rack filled with flickering lights.

"You should say a prayer," the older woman whispers. "You know, something like 'St. Jude, please help so and so in his or her hour of need,' something heartfelt like that. There's no particular way of doing it. I'm sure you'll do fine."

"How is Hillary?" Dr. Norm says.

"I'm not suppose to talk about that."

"That's okay, Fiorella."

"Miss Hillary tells me, I'm sorry."

"It's okay, really. I try to respect a person's boundaries."

Dr. Norm bows his head in front of his just lighted candle. *"How do I make my way through to you? How do other people get you to listen?"* He is thinking his prayer, keeping it to himself. This isn't what he does, hardly ever. He's praying, *"Let's get this bastard, okay? This is one dangerous son-of-a-bitch. Are you getting this? How's the reception? Let me say it again. Dear God, let me get this bastard."*

144

SO MUCH FOR
BEING A NICE GUY

On the Way to Vitoria
April 21nd, Present

GRIGOR CAN'T STOP the fantasies. He wants to roast Hillary slowly the way people roast pigs. Crank that bitch round and round and hear her juices hiss. Smell the sweet skin as it goes crispy. *Mmm-mm, chard goodness. Pass me a plate of that.* Dr. Bolian now has Hillary Ann Tucker on his ever expanding To-Do list. Nobody tells a *physician* to get out of a patient's room at gun point.

Grigor has a window seat on the train going from Madrid to Vitoria-Gasteiz – a three and a half hour, 227 km ride, according to the conductor, who's got the dull look of an escapee from a retirement community. The train's interior is spotless, beige and dark green, the lighting coming from some hidden place above him. Bolian loves trains. He can look out the window and watch the farms and houses and countryside and all the assholes going about their pathetic, insignificant business.

"That cretin waved a fucking gun in your face." The Commander is in Grigor's head again. He hears the Gipper's outrage. That old west schoolmarm scolding, how Ronny used to do with the Russians and the democrats. *"And you do nothing, do you? Isn't that right? You should've grabbed the damn gun and straightened her out."*

The insults play over and over.

It's Ron the Relentless, but he is relentless for Grigor

145

Bolian's own good, always that. The Commander has everyone's interest at heart. That's the mark of the Gipper, his Gipperesque nature.

Talking Points that enrage: 1) the pistol in his face. 2) Hillary telling him when he can come to see the great and holy and totally fucked up Raymond Mack and when it's off limits. *"You don't come here any time you want, Bolian. Visiting hours apply."* 3) The bitch's all business façade behind her prissy two-toned pistol. *Something anyone can do if you have a pistol,* he thinks. *What's the big deal about that?* 4) Hillary's Just "Can't Help Loving My Man" attitude. That truly irritates Grigor, beyond every reason. It's the alpha and the omega of his rage. He remembers her in the Village, *circa* 1996, when the two of them were fucking each other like gerbils on acid.

Who can trust a bitch? Seriously.

"Mister, is it okay I sit here?" The girl must be nine or ten, a small, bony thing with tan skin and large black eyes, maybe she's Spanish, maybe Indian or Pakistani. *Who the shit can tell nowadays?* Such an exquisite face, though, so delicate, so flawless, as if Katharine Hepburn had mated with some Bollywood star and produced a tiny beast with Cut-your-Finger cheekbones and a polite disposition, something made on one of God's better days. The girl says her name is Sofia. Then she says, "Mother tells people I have very good manners."

Dr. Bolian doesn't care if the child is nice. He's decided to travel incognito and only gives a nod back. He has on a Navy Blue NY baseball cap and Ray-Ban Wayfarers, his Kennedy-DiMaggio look, an oldie but a goodie reference.

"Momma wants both seats," Sofia says. "Her feet get swollen. People need to stretch out when they have swollen feet. Are you in the movies?"

Grigor doesn't answer. He settles deeper into his seat,

head against the window and ready to nap.

"Movie stars wear baseball caps and sunglasses," the girl says.

"—You caught me." Grigor is still leaning against the window, eyes closed.

"*Truly?* Oh *God*." Her accent definitely from some part of Massachusetts. Sofia has become very animated. "I knew it, I *knew*. Mama will be *mucho* jealous. What's your name, what movies?"

Grigor skips the name part; instead, he says, "You know the movie with the old naked woman tied to the bed? With scarves. Very pretty scarves, different colors? And I mean she's really *old*. The one where the guy gives her mushroom tea?"

"...I-I think so." No, she doesn't. But she really wants to. Sofia is looking down at her lap, perhaps putting the scarves and the mushroom tea together.

Dr. Bolian goes on, glances at her and shuts his eyes again. "But the mushroom tea is this poisonous psychedelic stuff? Where people get totally messed up and get bad cramps and die slowly?"

"...Okay, *okay*." Sofia's voice brightens. The "poisonous" detail about the tea makes all the difference – well, sort of – and her attitude goes from doubt to very close to sure. "—Mushrooms. Yeah, all *right*, I remember."

"Well I was the guy."

"—You? You were *that* guy?"

"—Uh-huh."

"God, you were the mushroom guy."

"What are the chances of that?"

"I can't believe I'm sitting next to the mushroom guy."

"—Hey, your lucky day." Grigor sits up, studies her for a second or two behind his tortoise shell Wayfarers and grins. He says, "Later in the movie I kill this slimeball lawyer. We're drinking at this outdoors café, middle of the morning, and I – I should say, 'my character' – anyway, I just get up and go behind him, slit his throat and walk away." Grigor snaps his fingers. "—Just walk away, little girl. What'd you think of that?"

"—Oh, wow. *Wicked.*"

The doctor thinks about the word "wicked" and nods slowly, sincerely. "Yes, I think you've captured it. 'Wicked,' to be sure."

Dr. Bolian is now contemplating how he might become a folk hero, have a band of boys and girls who adore him. No, no. *Worship* him. *How delightful, how wonderfully delightful. My children. My followers. My darling little elves.* Then Grigor could go over to Hillary Ann Tucker's house and slit her fucking throat.

WAITING ON DEATH

Pamplona
April 21ⁿᵈ

TEN-TWENTY-TWO in the morning and they are inside
the Poco Bull Café having tapas – *Plato de Queso Y
Carne*: cheeses, smoked meats, fig jam and hot fresh
bread. Isaac is wolfing down the bread. *Like there's no
tomorrow*, he thinks. Then he thinks, *Like a last meal* and
cringes at the thought.

"—Slow down," Lili says. She's having her morning red
and some sort of sweet and crumbly goat cheese.
"Seriously. You'll choke. How you doin', anyway?"

"I feel like I'm in one of those prison movies." Isaac
picks up a piece of the goat cheese, sniffs it, makes a face,
and puts it back on the tray. He says, "You know, *Dead
Man Walking*, that type of thing. Did you ever see that
one? Shawn Penn as the almost dead guy and Susan
Sarandon as the nun?" Isaac didn't wait for an answer. "I
used to say to myself, 'Who the fuck can eat when they're
going to die?' Know what I mean? The concept of a last
meal never made sense. But I was wrong, actually."

"—Not you."

"It can happen, believe me."

The morning is chilly and wet and the front window of
the café is streaked with rain. There is a polished
mahogany wood bar with a brass railing to rest your foot.
The tables are small and round, draped in white linen. A
shadowy room lighted by candles no matter what time of
day, no matter the weather. Isaac Stalin likes the place but
wishes the shadows were bigger and darker.

"—everybody dies, Isaac."

149

He takes a quick swig of the wine then spreads fig jam over his third piece of bread. "Says the woman who nobody wants to kill. *Nobody*. You can afford to be cavalier, Lili. Nobody's after you're ass. It's amazing how nonchalant a person can be if they're not in the line of fire. Let's face it, some guy's father isn't dying and wants old scores settled. Which, by the way, must be *so* nice."

"Did you forget I almost died."

"That's very different."

"—Since when?"

"You get what I mean," Isaac tells her. He's looking at his now empty wine glass and thinking he better have a refill.

"No, no. I don't *get* shit." She's becoming very pissy. She says, "I always thought dead was dead. Crazy me, right? But in case you missed the bulletin, dead *is* dead. It doesn't matter how you get there."

"Your asshole father hired a guy to kill me."

Lili whispers each word separately. "I. Almost. Died." She cups her palm over Isaac's hand. Her fingers are warm and he feels a little of the tension leave his neck and arms. She says, "You're not alone, okay? I'll call my father. We'll straighten it out."

"You'd do that?"

"Why wouldn't I do that?"

Isaac nods; thinking, *Yeah, okay, why wouldn't she?* He saved her life. He settled the score. Any sane, reasonable person could see that. *Saving a person's life has got to count for something, no matter how big a jerk I was back in the day. It's not like I killed her family, or burned down her house, what-have-you. I'm your regular jerk. Everybody gets to be a jerk at least once in their lives, right?*

"I'm sure daddy would respect my wishes," Lili says. She is spreading a knife-tip of goat cheese on a piece of bread. "I mean he's very stubborn, no question. It's never a walk in the park with him. And it's always more about him than *my* wishes, but you just have to be firm, you know? Daddy respects that – if he's really concerned about my business, then he'll have to listen. You know what I'm saying? He's got to know the world doesn't revolve around him."

"Lots of luck with that."

"We need to go on with our walk, too."

"Are you kidding?" Isaac is pouring some of the red in his glass and shaking his head "—Absolutely not."

"—*Isaac*."

"Hey. Don't give me 'Isaac,' okay? It's not your life."

"You don't think he can kill us here?" Lili is looking at him like he's a crazy man. "—Or *Any*where. In our room, in our bed? You could be sitting on the toilet and he wouldn't knock. What I'm saying is, this person is a professional. He doesn't give a crap where you are or what time of day or night it is. He doesn't care."

"That's comforting."

"Oh stop it," Lili says. "You know what I mean. There is no place to hide.

And *because* there's no place to hide, we go about our business. Since he can kill us anywhere, we don't let him screw with our lives. We just need to be, you know, vigilant."

"The 'if you panic, the terrorists win' strategy?"

"—Pre*ci*sely."

"That's just fucking stupid. Call you're father."

BUYING LOCALLY

Santiago
April 21, Evening

WHY CARRY INTERNATIONALLY, *when you can buy locally?* The wisdom of Dr. Norm's grad student, Lydia Pepper, or probably her father. Pearlman is staring at the red-rust double doors of an apartment off the Plaza de los Platerias. This is the address Lydia's father had given her, where to buy a firearm in Santiago. *How does the guy know that?* Norman likes to imagine Daddy Desmond with a six-shooter tied to the thigh of, maybe, buckskinned jeans, a gunslinger from the old school.

The afternoon after their Buy Locally discussion, Lydia had knocked on his office door with the note.

"Daddy wants me to give you this," the girl had said. She'd handed him a folded piece of yellow legal paper with the handwritten address of a Santiago gun dealer on it. Lydia wore cut off denims. The girl was short, five-two or three, and she had the legs of a NFL quarterback but without the hair. Then Lydia said, "I told him why you were going to Spain, and he made a few calls."

"Oh jeez that's far too much trouble," Immediately Dr. Norm let the guilt settle in. *Hello, darkness, my old friend.* Favors from strangers are never good things. "Your dad had to do a lot Out of the Way stuff, didn't he? A person has to call this one and that one. A person has to call the place itself and find out if they got what was discussed, an automatic pistol of some type."

"—A Glock 17 Gen 4."

"Yes, yes, that one." Norm didn't know a Glock 17 Gen 4 from whatever, his foot. He was more concerned how he'd inconvenienced a stranger. "What did it cost him to call Spain?"

'It doesn't matter."

"Of course it matters. I'll reimburse him."

"—Don't worry."

"Allow me to worry. People have limited incomes."

"It took him five minutes," Lydia said. He could hear the weariness in her voice. She had her blond hair pulled straight back and tied with a thick red rubber band. The blond color gave way to darker hair at the root. She said, "He loves this shit, believe me. Woops. Excuse the language, professor."

"— Please. 'Shit' is a perfectly acceptable word. I don't use it too much myself, but people should talk like they talk."

"Well he loves doing this shit," she said again.

"Thank him for me." Dr. Norm took her hand in both of his and shook it. Her skin felt warm and damp. "Don't forget, okay? You think you can remember that? Tell him I'm appreciative of the, um, shit he went through to get the information."

"—No problem."

"—Good, good."

Lydia had lifted herself on her tiptoes and kissed his cheek. She smiled one of the oddest smiles Dr. Norm had ever seen and turned on her heels and jogged-walk out the office.

So that was then and this is now.

Norman Pearlman is watching one of the red-rust double doors open. He's still in front of the apartment off the Plaza de los Platerias. Dr. Norm makes his way into the shadowy room and waits for his eyes to adjust to the dimness. *Oh my God*, he thinks. Maybe he even says it out loud, he's not sure. The shock of what he is seeing is like an outer body experience. Or what Dr. Norm imagines when he imagines an outer body experience.

The room is filled with guns. Firearms. Whatever you're suppose to call them. There's a rocket launcher reclining on a forest green, two-seater Victorian. He's seen weapons like this one on the news shows, things that take down airplanes. Usually one man with a checkered scarf wrapped about his head has raised the launcher thing with one hand while the other men surrounding him jump up and down and wave their arms in the air.

"I am Goyo," the man says, a soft, pleasant voice. He walks from the shadows and bows to Dr. Norm. The man is thin and small and wears a silk white suit. His hair is a black and gray mix, neatly trimmed and slicked straight back. "You are...?"

"Dr. Pearlman."

"Of course, forgive. Mr. Pepper's friend, yes?"

"—Not exactly friends, but he's a fine man." Norm has to squint to see anything beyond the rocket launcher and Goyo.

"Lincoln was a fine man," Goyo says. "Mr. Pepper is a man among men. A protector, if you understand. My English isn't the best. "

"Your English is excellent."

"—Like the Templars. You know the Templars."

"I do," Norm Pearlman says. Goyo is getting a small tan wood case from the glass coffee table. The wood case has a polished brass lock. Norm says, "They were called the 'poor knights of Christ' – a sort of religious-military order."

"I'm impressed, Dr. Pearlman." Goyo opens the wood box and shows the dark Glock on its red velvet cushion. "Very good, I see why Mr. Pepper went to the trouble of approaching this humble salesman. The Templar's job was to protect Christian pilgrims traveling to the holy land. Such an awesome task. Do you understand?"

"—Oh, yes. Very well."

CALLS BEST LEFT UNANSWERED

Hospital Universitario de Madrid
April 22nd, Morning

"TELL ME THE name of your daughter."

"—Who's this?"

"I will murder her right here on the street." The man's voice was steady, close to a whisper. "Again. What's your daughter's name?"

"I'm hanging up now." Raymond Mack can't believe he's getting a call like this. Who calls a person inches away from death with this sort of shit? And *non*-amusing shit, by the way. Some totally non-amusing shit from some totally non-amusing asshole. Ray says, "I'm in a hospital, you son of bitch."

"—Her name, Raymond."

"I'm hanging up."

"Yeah, you do that," the man says, his voice still a whisper. "Hang up on me. Of course I'll have to come over tonight and cut off your dick."

"—W-What?"

"And after I cut off your little friend, I'll shove it down your throat. Bet that won't be the first time, will it, Ray? Ever seen a castration? You bleeding all over the place, blood's everywhere. You'll try to hold yourself, you know, try top stop it. But there's nothing there to hold – no there *there*, so-to-speak. We're talking phantom penis, Ray – like phantom limb. There's phantom penis, too. Bet you didn't know–"

Raymond Mack hangs up the phone.

The monitor is beeping. Both his blood pressure and heart rate are climbing. He looks over his left shoulder at the monitor. His pressure is 210/197. The night shift nurse runs into the dark room, looks at the neon green numbers and mutters, "Oh, Jesus." She is the stocky one with the thick ankles, Somebody Rodriguez. She taps a manicure, polished red fingertip at the monitor, hoping everything will go back to manageable. It doesn't.

Rodriguez mutters "Oh, Jesus," again and says to her patient, "What's going on here, Mr. Mack?"

"—Bad dream."

"Must've been the bad dream of bad dreams." She's ready going out the door; saying, "I'm getting you Ativan."

Raymond looks at the beige phone on the nightstand. The Venetian blinds are half open and moonlight goes through the slits and across the phone and his bed sheets and up the white wall to his right.

Who the fuck are you? Raymond Mack thinks. *Who calls and says such things?* First Isaac Stalin comes to mind but that asshole is already with his daughter. Then Ray begins to imagine the caller appearing at the window. In this fantasy the window opens and the Venetian blinds are pushed aside. The moonlight light is very bright and hides the intruder's face. Yet, yet. He can see the smile. It's stretched across a hidden face, big and wide. Funny what you think, *God, who is your dentist, friend? That's a movie star smile, the sort of smile that can earn a man a living.* Ray imagines swooning women. Imagines mommies holding up their babies for kissing. A smile like that can rotate the earth. Then moonlight flashes off a smooth, polished thing in the man's hand.

The phone is ringing again, more a buzz than a ring, hushed but insistent. Ray can hear the beeps of his monitor quicken; the beat of his heart, too. His hand hovers over the receiver before he answers.

"—Lili," the man on the other end says. He says it in that steady, whispery voice.

Raymond keeps quiet.

"That's her name," the man says. "I'm right, aren't I?"

"...Leelee."

"—What? I can't hear you, Ray."

"It's pronounced 'Leelee,' not 'Lily' ... you moron."

"You think I don't *know* that?" the man's whisper has become more throaty, more disturbing. Abruptly he shifts, his laugh soft, easy. "Well, my goodness. Look at us two, old hens bickering over the same egg."

Raymond can hear the goddamn machine next to him picking up the beat. He is sure his heart is going to break through his chest, explode and turn the white walls and ceiling red.

"...what the fuck," Ray says.

"That's what I'm going to do to her before I kill her."

"Who is this?"

"A disgruntled employee."

Quiet.

"...Ray?"

Quiet.

The sound of the monitor had shifted from a beeping noise to a single, unending note.

WATCHING THEM

GRIGOR BOLIAN HAD watched them on the road, tracking Ray's daughter and Isaac Stalin for a day or two – Puente La Reina to Estella, Los Arcos to Navarrete.

Dr. Bolian is now looking out the window of his room in the Hotel San Amalia, a lovely hotel with just a hint of euro-trash. That's how Grigor sees this room, a dandelion in the wood. Look at its silky azure-colored wallpaper, its white Victoria headboard and bedcover, its red brocaded furniture.

"—Like a Spanish whore who pretends virtue," The Commander whispers.

"That's it, perfectly," Grigor whispers back. It's talk that only the doctor hears.

"Nothing like a fine Spanish whore," The Commander says in his shaky-headed, wobbly drawl. "And if you can't get a Spaniard, a Mexican'll do. Good people, the Mexicans. I've known a few."

"—In the biblical sense," Grigor adds.

That one gets a laugh.

Grigor loves following Lili and the closet fag Isaac Stalin. The doc waits for them on the trail, hides behind big rocks or a cluster of trees. Occasionally he makes a pistol out of his thumb and index finger – aiming at them as they pass – and pulling the trigger.

"... kapow," he says to himself.

Total fucking fun.

Dr. Bolian even left a message for Lili at one of the hostels. In a sealed envelope, of course. The message read:

I killed your father, bitch. Next it's you and the gay gentleman. Are you really fucking him? What does that say about you?

He wishes he could've seen her face. But, hey, if wishes were candy we'd all be diabetic.

They look around a lot, Lili and Closet Boy. He's watching them with binoculars from his hotel room window. Tourists, townies, the occasional car or truck, any of this will spark discussions between them that appear both secretive and anxious.

"Our two crazy kids darn well know what's up," The Commander says. *"You can't fool the smart ones."*

"It's so very exciting."

Dr. Bolian also prides himself on such observations. With all reverence to The Commander, a person doesn't need the blinding love and votes of a nation to get it. Who doesn't thrill to the sight of people waiting to die? Yes, the cat has definitely shredded the shit out of the bag.

"You're captivated," The Commander says.

"—Better than sex."

"Do you mean watching it or doing it?"

"—Both."

The Commander gives his rare, full-throated belly laugh. He can't help himself. A funny man is a funny man.

Grigor feels honored, his cheeks blush hot. To make the Great One laugh, not trivial stuff.

"How will you kill them?" The Commander wants to know. *"Let me hear the juicy, step by step details."*

This is a problem.

He's not sure how he will do his job. Or "jobs" with an "s." There is Lili, there is Closet Boy, and let's not forget Hillary Ann Tucker. Hill and Lili are kills, perhaps done the way he'd handled Jake Wheatfield, the lawyer – mushrooms and a knife, an argument can be made for consistency, a flamboyant signature that catches the imagination. These kills would establish who's in charge of what. Both deaths say, *I bow to none*. The bitch pulled a gun on him – on *him*. Who the fuck in his or her respective right mind does that shit? Who in his or her right mind would ever, ever let that shit go?

Nobody. No-fucking-body.

That's rule number uno, he thinks. *You do not fuck with me, I fuck with YOU. That's the rule of rules. The Golden Rule, if you will. The rule people measure.* "Can he back it up?" *they say, or maybe they contemplate it as they watch the play unfold.* "Can he be a hundred percent real? Will he kill whoever he has to kill to not lose his place, to not lose the fear and respect of others?

Grigor Bolian says a big "Yes, I Can" to that one.

Kill Hill for the gun in his face. Kill Hill for dismissing the betters days of his life. How stupid of him to think she would remember their time together the way he'd remembered it. Their Village days, he called it, starting with Kara Nissim's party in May of '96 and ending in late June of that same year. Less than two months. Who remembers less than two months of anything?

I did ... I do.

To see no recognition on her face, to see only that Pico automatic, the sting of it surprised him. No, crushed him. *You murdered me long ago*, he thinks. *And you don't even acknowledge us by remembering the crime.*

Then there's Isaac. Paid to kill Closet Boy, paid to let him go – a problem fit for Solomon. He will follow Jake Wheatfield's advice, *"My client isn't unreasonable. A wound is fine, a substantial wound is never frowned upon, Greg. Something that says you tried and almost succeeded."*

Why not cut off his delicate, pretty hands and cauterize his wrists? That would be substantial.

THERAPY AFTER DR. NORM

Glenside, Pennsylvania
March 15ᵗʰ, 1991

"STILL SO PRETTY," Margaret Ramirez says. "—How many years, twelve, thirteen – more? Something like that?"

"—Something like, yes."

"—So pretty."

Lili isn't sure how long it's been. But who cares, really? Lili has just escaped a too-many-year marriage to Norm Pearlman. This is therapy, not a class reunion. She and Margaret won't be exchanging pictures of their babies or telling each other who they almost fucked in their senior year.

Once again the social worker and her client sit across from each other on the same padded corduroy chairs, the cushions giving way more than remembered, the arms worn and starting to thread. Lili likes it that Margaret's office hasn't changed, the same second floor sandstone-colored office building, the windows showing the same little park with its gray dirt path and wood benches. Margaret's office has even kept that eerie forest green and floral wallpaper.

"I can't figure out why I married the guy," Lili says.

"How old were you then?"

"—Eighteen. Him, too."

"So three years after your therapy with me?"

"I dunno, I guess." Lili is starting to feel annoyed. Nowadays it doesn't take much. *My world doesn't revolve*

165

around you, she thinks. But if Lili's honest, she kind of knows it did and does. "...I-I felt unprotected. After I left here, I mean."

"So he's a kind man? Considerate?"

"—Yeah, I'll give him that."

"—Overweight?"

Lili already know where this is going. This pisses her off, too. "...yeah," she says, begrudgingly giving a little to Margaret. "I guess he could lose a few."

"—So at least as fat as me?" Unrelenting bitch.

"—Yeah, yeah."

"See where I'm going with this?"

"—Uh-huh, okay." Lili cannot help but smile. It's quick and gone but it's a smile all the same. This is why she's here, isn't it – to be human again in safe company, to be held tight by this woman's words, by the tone of her enduring presence? Lili says, "I still hate it when you're right."

"—It's probably not all hate."

"See. You're a gloater."

Yes, Dr. Norm is kind. Yes, Dr. Norm is fat. Yes, Dr. Norm is protective, at least he always made her feel safe and this during a time when Lili didn't feel safe at all. The way Isaac Stalin took her out of the Madrid competition those many years ago had changed her perception of the world. Life became a more dangerous journey, a journey cautiously played. The wet cold of that Christmas night hadn't left her. She remembered every detail, her plunge into the ice and logs that jammed the boy's backyard pool, the abrupt, head-jarring pain of the log smacking against her ear.

I could've died, for godsake.

Dr. Norm guarded Lili from her bad memories and her worse fantasies. Yet things with him were always a little too much. He was *too* kind, *too* fat, *too* protective, too, too,

too. Here's the truth, though, Norm Pearlman guarded her better then the Secret Service guarded the president, no question there, or better than she imagined the secret guarded the president. The man did everything but talk into his wrist and scan the area for clues.

That was Dr. Norm. *Is* him. Yesterday, today, tomorrow, the amazingly bizarre Dr. Norm. This man can pull shit from his ass and say the universe put it there – the stars, the planets, the gassy, cosmic clouds that nurse these things.

"The universe lets me know," he'd tell her.

Lili Mack has been gazing at her lap and talking. Now she looks up at Margaret, the social worker twenty pounds heavier than she remembers, hair white and clipped ear-length. Lili says, "When the bad days came, Norm had already prepared me. 'Watch out for a truck today – a bread truck,' he'd say. This could be a week, sometimes a month before the event. But damn if something didn't happen. The bread truck sure happened. That truck came out of nowhere and took my right, rear fender, just ripped it off. Scared the shit out of me."

"So your hubby's a kind man, attentive," Margaret listing his good points. "He protects you from the world. Or tries to. Oh and most important, he tells your future pretty accurately." Then she pauses before adding, "—And you left him?"

"Yeah, not fast enough," Lili says, nodding. "Crazy, huh?"

"Am I missing something?"

"You think I'd want to know, the future and what-have-you. But I don't, believe me. You wouldn't either. Nobody wants to see the train coming."

AMONG THE TOMBS

Cementerio de Nuestra Senora de la Almudena
April 28th, Afternoon

FIVE MILLION PEOPLE are buried at the Almudena.
It's the biggest City of the Dead in the world. The City
that Always Sleeps, Hillary Ann is thinking, amazed at the
row after row of gray and white stone sarcophagi. So many
are here, politicians, actors, singers, novelists, Nobel
laureates, academicians.

Today the American Artist Raymond Mack joins them.

Hill had discussed the dirtnap thing with Ray. Where
did he want to be interred? Did he want a coffin, or the fire
ride? Fire rides are cheaper and more environmentally
friendly. Mainly, though, where did he want the burial?
She never liked his answer. He kept telling her Spain.

"I just don't get you," she'd say. "You're an American,
Ray, first and forever, and a *famous* American. How's it
going to look?"

"What the fuck do I care." Ray's answer to most
things.

"Well you ought to care."

"Home is where the heart is, right? Am I right?" Who
could not agree with such a nugget. "I love Spain, love it.
Shoot me, okay? I love the bulls and the people and the
little cafés."

"It's so, I dunno, *un*-American."

"America'll get over it."

"That's it? 'America will get over it'? Really?"

Raymond had bought his coffin after the cancer
diagnosis. Then he painted bullfighting scenes on it.

So weird to see, Hill thinks. *Who does that shit?*

She's seated near his open grave site, amid large cypress trees, with fifty or so other mourners. Painted onto the coffin's mahogany sides are twisters of sand. Bulls are hunched and ready to charge. The matadors all look like Raymond, their capes unfurled, whipped by a breeze. Thousands of dollars are about to be buried in the ground to rot. More than one of the artist's bereaved friends advises Hill to put Baby Ray's body in something else, anything else, fucking Tupperware, and sell the painted coffin.

"God, you could like retire, girl," Chloe Remme whispers, Hill's new BFF, a tall, skinny blonde who works clerical at the embassy. Chloe stands half in the shade and half in the sunshine. She has on a silky black pants suit and wide-brim hat, a laced veil shadows her face. The young woman says, "That's the most beautiful coffin I've ever seen. You want to throw dirt on that?"

"I'm really going to miss him." Hill's been crying for days. She feels her throat constrict just speaking the words. "...shit, shit."

"—Hey, c'mon now," her BFF says in a soft voice.

"I'm sorry."

"Don't be *sorry*." Chloe rolls her eyes. Like unbelievable. Like who apologizes for *that*. "We love who we love, you know? Who can help such a thing? I wish I'd find somebody to love me that much, to love me enough to cry. All I find are assholes. I'm serious. If there's only one asshole in the room, I'll find him. I'm like a finely tuned asshole magnet. And these guys all think *I'm* the moron. Me. Did you ever have a truly dumb guy explain things to you? Like *I'm* the dumb one?"

"—Oh not you," Hill says, her interest elsewhere.

"Oh, yes, me. Ms. Stupid Shit. That's what they think."

Hill is studying the paintings on the sides and top of the coffin and puts a finger to her lips, hoping Chloe will shut up or at least tone it down.

This part of the cemetery is at a higher elevation. The wind flutters the green and white awning spread above the grave and the mourners who are seated on wood fold-out chairs. The sky has long heavy clouds and the rain comes and goes. The spring in Spain reminds Hillary of Seattle, all breezy and gray.

... the rain in Spain.

"Funerals always scare me," Chloe says, leaning toward Hill, her voice wispy and with a tremor. "I imagine myself inside the coffin, you know? Like it's me in there and I know it's me and I can't get out. What's worse, no matter how loud I yell, nobody hears me."

"They first take out all your organs."

"—What?"

"I'm just saying, don't worry about it."

Hillary doesn't want to deal with Chloe. Hillary is struggling with who she's supposed to be. Is there such a thing as a "widowed girlfriend?" She was nothing special before hooking up with Ray. Now that he's being tossed into the ground, does she return to being nobody special? Hill wishes she'd married the guy. Raymond certainly wanted to get married; talked about it every chance he got. But her anxiety had stopped her. A talented guy like that, he would've tossed her off, become tired of her. All that beauty crap only takes you so far.

After the funeral Hillary says goodbye to her freaked out, empty-eyed BFF and begins a solo walk through the cypress trees and the gray afternoon, toward her parked Rover.

This is where Hill feels an arm wrap about her upper chest and shoulders from behind. She's jerked backwards, her shoulder blades tight to the person's chest. Then a hand is pressing across her mouth. She's being dragged into the shadows of the cypress trees.

"—My sympathies," a man's voice says, his breath on her ear. Peppermint? Something like peppermint. Strange what you think. Is he chewing gum? Maybe a mint? He says, "This'll just take a minute."

There is a sharp, hard sting on both sides of her neck. Hill looks down and sees the front of her dark coat go slick and wet.

LILI AND ISAAC SEE THE WRITING ON THE WALL

Tosantos, Spain
April 28th, Late afternoon

"WELL I SAW *some*body," Isaac says.

"You sound like a crazy person." Lili Mack is trying to do a pencil sketch of the 9th century Ermita de Nuestra Señora de la Peña. The church was built into the side of a mountain. Dark openings clutter its face. Dug out windows, maybe. Or doors, but to where, to what end? Tosantos has long stretches of green farmland. There are houses with rococo rooftops and brick and stucco sides, some well kept, some in ruin. Lili says, "This is such a *gor*geous area." She continues to draw but waves a free hand above her head to indicate where Isaac should look. "Try not to be so down in the mouth," she says. "You never enjoy yourself."

"Hey. A guy's going to kill me."

"You need to calm down," Lili is shading the drawing the way her father taught her, slanting the pencil and giving it quick, even strokes.

"You aren't concerned?"

"Of course I'm concerned."

"How'd you feel if it was you?" Isaac Stalin puts his hand atop Lili's and stops her sketching. "It's easier because it's me, isn't it? I'm the one he's after. I'm the one who has to do the worrying."

Lili can't believe him. "You think I'm *not* worried? You think I'm going, 'Oh gosh, sure glad it's asshole Isaac and not me. I'm so lucky.' Is that what you think?"

"Yeah, pretty much."

"It's unbelievable. You can be such a moron."

"It's a question," a weariness in his voice.

"No it's not. A question is, 'Listen, Lili, what can we do to protect each other from this insane shit?' That's a question. Or 'Listen, Lili, you think we should go our separate ways? I don't want you getting hurt.' Something like that. A person who loves someone is thinking about himself, sure, but he's also thinking about the person he's with, how he can protect that person."

"So I should think about you?"

"—About *us.*"

"So you're saying I should go off by myself?" Isaac looks down and touches the new bandage on his right knee, the place where he scraped himself a few days ago. Lili had cleaned and bandaged the wound this morning. Isaac says, "I got gangrene. If this guy doesn't kill me first, my leg will probably drop off, anyway."

"You don't have gangrene."

"I got something."

"You're right there. But not gangrene."

They are sitting next to one another on the grass as Lili sketches the church. The ruins of a two-story farm house is behind them, the roof caved into the second floor. A cloudless blue sky today, the first once since their trip began.

Lili slips her sketchbook and pencil back into her knapsack. She stands and rubs a fist into the small of her back. "I think we should go see that thing," nodding toward the mountain. "How often do we get to see a 9th century church in a mountain? Like never, right?"

"That's an unnecessary half mile."

"Mr. Enthusiasm."

"I'm not saying I *won't* go." He's calling after her,

waving one hand, the other over his brow to block the sun. "*Hey*. Don't be that way. *Hey*. We should conserve our energy, that's all I'm saying. Li? Hey, Li. You're one stubborn person, you know that? I got a wound here."

Lili is already heading toward the mountain and the weirdest church ever. Who wouldn't want to get a closer look? She's annoyed at Isaac, at the situation, at the way things are getting in between her and what *could* be an interesting time – an out and out good time. And ok, yes, he *did* save her life. Saving somebody's life has to wipe away past grievances. Any clear thinking person should agree with that, particularly teenage stuff. God think about it. Adolescents are hormonally psychotic for at least six or seven years. Save a person's life and it sort of puts an end to the smaller shit, doesn't it? Ok, yes, *and* a lot of it is her fault. She'll admit that. Lili isn't giving herself a free ride in all of this. She's the one who got swept away by her father's outrage. Poor little Lili Mack. Boo Hoo. What's wrong with teaching kids music? She likes her job at Germantown High. What about a little more patience with the guy who saved her life? What about that? What about growing the fuck up?

"—Hey, hey." Isaac is hobble-running after her.

Lili stops, turning toward him, waiting as he walks up to her. She puts a hand on his shoulder and nudges him to her, kissing his cheek.

"W-What're you doing?" He draws away slightly.

"I *am* concerned," she says, her voice soft, just for him. "—Concerned about you. About us. I know we're in trouble. Believe me, I do know. I get that my paranoid father wanted a 'you can run but you can't hide' situation. That's so like daddy. But I just handle anxiety different than you, that's all."

When they finally enter Ermita de Nuestra Señora de la Peña together, Isaac has his arm about her waist. The inside of the mountain looks cut or blasted into an arched room or worship area of gray and white stone. The pews have cushioned seats and brass filigree backs. Fresh flowers surround the pulpit and lighted candles are everywhere.

"God this is beautiful," Lili whispers.

"...yeah." He's looking somewhere else.

"—What's wrong?"

Isaac is staring at the wall to their right – and nods.

Words are printed in charcoal on the rough stone. Lili Mack presses the flat of her hand to her mouth.

hi Isaac hi Lili

you guys having fun?

DR. NORM'S PARALLEL LIFE

Burgos, Spain
April 28th , Early evening

APARTMENTS OVER THE little shops are mostly long and narrow windows framed in red and white painted wood. Dr. Norm is walking the narrow gray street with its wide brick sidewalks and street lamps. The lights have just come on and tourists are everywhere, particularly the shops and the cafés.

Burgos is part of The Way of St. James. Lili Mack has to pass through Burgos on her way to the Cathedral Santiago de Compostela. Could Lili die before then, before she and her friend reached Burgos?

Yes, there's a possibility. *Nothing is set in stone*, he thinks.

But the *probability* value is low, in the thirty-two to forty-eight percentile range. Dr. Norm has determined that the level of probability rises the closer Lili, her friend and the assassin travel to the finish line, the cathedral. This is based on "preferred" outcomes. Unfortunately, preferred outcomes are mostly an educated guess based each variable's history – how it has acted in the past – and, of course, the person doing the statistic.

There is also another problem.

Norm has been hearing his mother's voice since 3:47 in the afternoon. He'd looked at his wristwatch and wrote the exact time in a pocket-sized notepad. He is not at the top of his game.

Norm used to hallucinate his mother's voice during his late teens, early twenties. It began a couple of months after his father had punched his mom one too many times and sent her to the hospital with a broken jaw. Most of these beatings happened late at night. Norm could hear the sobs and shouting coming from their bedroom. On the night Harry Pearlman broke his wife's jaw, the angry bastard had freaked himself out enough to pack his old army duffle bag and depart their lives for good.

This recent reoccurrence of his mom's voice probably had to do with Lili Mack. The similarity between the two events hasn't escaped him.

"You're saving her over and over again, aren't you?" How many therapists have told him that? The relationship between other woman and his mom were obvious. He'd been too young and too afraid to protect his mother from his dad's abuse and the guilt had been batting him around for years. One of his many therapists had said, "On the positive side, women are lucky to have you around."

His mother's name is Grace – *was* Grace. Today her ghost is either whimpering or calling to him, or both, the noise distant but frantic.

"...*shhh*, mama," he whispers. No one's there, obviously.

"Don't let him hurt me, Norm."

"Daddy's gone now, mama. He's been gone for years."

Harry Pearlman had worked security for a chemical/ fertilizer company in South Philly. He'd been retired from the military for six months and the job supplemented his pension. Harry was a short man, five-three, five-five, with thick arms and legs and a neck the size of a child's waist. If you had any sense at all, you knew you didn't go looking for a round or two with Pearlman. His father didn't drink but he did have red in the face temper issues. Since the man's return to civilian life nightly marital arguments were common.

Bruises had begun appearing on Grace's neck and arms.

His mother was screaming that night and there were sounds of a thing snapping against flesh. The boy had taken his father's .38 from its holster hooked on the mahogany hall tree in the foyer. Norm intended to walk into his parents' bedroom and shoot the old man. His hands were wet and shaky and he he'd dropped the gun. This lead to an event Norm would've preferred to forget. A round went off and blew away part of the little toe on his right foot.

Now Dr. Norm is imagining his dead mother' voice, again.

"—Save me," his mother is saying. "You're father's here."

"Calm down, please. Okay?"

Norm isn't a fool. He sees the tourists and the locals looking at him. He knows they are concerned about his behavior. No one likes it when strangers talk to invisible beings. People become frightened, some talk to the policia and point to him. He's had six conversations with the Burgos policia today.

His mother is screaming, only Norm can hear it. *If a tourist looks at you, just smile.* Grace is far away, how she sounded when he was a child and upstairs in his dark bedroom.

"He's got the razor strap." Grace's saying; this between the breaths and the whimpers.

"It's not real, mama." Had he ever convinced her?

"I know when I'm being hit."

"Watch some TV. Get your mind off things."

"He's on the TV, too."

"Who's on the TV?"

"—Your *father*." She's totally exasperated with her

child, this gallant boy who does nothing but protects her. Doesn't he see anything? "Who do you think?" his mom says. "You *do* remember your crazy father, yes? Are you paying attention?"

"He left us, remember?" He tells her that on the streets of Burgos. "He's been gone for awhile."

"—So you say." Not believing him for a second.

Norman Pearlman's dad used to shave with a straight razor and he'd sharpen it on a long strip of oiled leather. Back and forth, back and forth. He'd beat Norm's mom with that strap when she wasn't listening to him, or if she said something stupid, or if she looked at him in an unpleasant way.

Harry, Laugh a Minute Harry. That's what people actually called him. No one could tell a joke like Harry Pearlman. "Harry, hon, you should be in show business," they'd say, all the ladies in the neighborhood; the ones in the bars, particularly. "You are funny as shit, Harry. You know that?"

Space-time is flexible for Dr. Norm. Parallel worlds shift and turn without his permission.

What world are you in today?

It's a question Dr. Norm asks him himself in the twisted sheets of every new morning. He will usual peek between the Venetian blinds, not sure of what is waiting for him. Have the cars changed? Are the trees still green? Do men and women still walk on two legs or is one good enough now? He's never fucking sure of anything, takes nothing for granted. There are mornings that he is too terrified to take a peek at all. On those days, he listens. Mumble, mumble. What the hell is this world saying to him? Which of the infinite worlds is saying it?

Norm Pearlman has seated himself outdoors at a Café. The tables and chairs are red plastic, the awning above him gray. He orders a carafe of chardonnay and bread and cheese. Norm is a big cheese man, in this or any world.

"Why do you have a gun?" his mother says.

He doesn't answer. His mother has followed him to the café. This has not been an easy day.

"*Nor*man, I'm talking."

"—To save my ex," he whispers.

"The bitch who left your marriage?"

"I'm not discussing her with you."

"Don't shoot yourself, again," Grace says.

FIORELLA DELIVERS THE NEWS

Burgos, Spain
April 29th, Mid-morning

"I CALLED MANY hostels, Senorita." The woman
sounds out of breath as if she'd been running from
hostel to hostel instead of using the phone.

Less than a minute ago the skinny young bearded man
who owns the God's Mercy Hostel pointed Lili Mack in the
direction of a black wall phone near the front desk.

"—For you. Some woman." He'd pointed without
glancing up from the folded paperback he was reading, an
old Kurt Vonnegut something.

Lili turns away from the man now, the receiver in
place, an index finger pressed to her free ear to block the
noise, and she says, "—I'm sorry, who's this?"

"—Fiorella," the woman tells her. She takes an audible
breath; then calms her voice, "I thought I'd never find you.
How lucky I am, how relieved. I work for Mr. Mack and
Miss Hillary. Or I used to work for them."

"Did they fire you?" Lili isn't sure why this woman
would be calling her. Did she want the daughter of the
man who fired her to get her job back?

"No, Senorita–"

"—Lili."

"No, Miss Lili. They no fire me, I'm a good worker. Mr.
Mack always says so.

Every time Mr. Mack comes to Madrid, he hires me
back. I work for him maybe fifteen years, maybe longer."

"So you quit working for him then?" Lili still couldn't figure out the reason for the call. Fiorella? Is that what she called herself? "—Is that it, Fiorella?"

The woman didn't answer.

Fifteen years is a very long time. Why hadn't her dad mentioned the name of his housekeeper? But then again why should he? The guy isn't a story teller, he's a painter. He *shows* his stories. If she wanted to know about Spain or the other places he traveled, she just needed to look at his work. So, no, her father didn't talk about his time in Spain – or anywhere else, for that matter.

He would give her a phone number, though. "For emergencies only," he'd tell her, always very emphatic about that. *The big deal artist Raymond Mack is also one of the great compartmentalizers*, she thinks. How many times did she have to interrogate him for just simple stuff – did he meet anybody? Things like that.

"—Are you still there, Fiorella?"

"Yes, Miss Lili."

"Listen, I don't mean to rush you," Lili says and again turns. This time to the tan stucco wall and away from a large, middle-aged guy with camouflage shorts and pink sunburned legs. The guy had pantomimed holding an imaginary phone while mouthing the words, *"Are you going to be long?"*

The whole pilgrim's hostel thing was losing its magic.

She says to Fiorella, "I'm on a public phone. We must take care of our business quickly." Why would this woman track her on the *Camino de Santiago*? What sort of person takes on such a job? "Can you hear me, Fiorella?"

"Yes, Miss Lili. You say I must hurry."

"Can you do that?"

"Yes, Miss Lili. You're father and Miss Hillary have passed."

"—What's that?" Lili turns to give the guy in the

camouflage shorts a Back the Fuck Off stare. Then she shoos him with an abrupt wave of her hand. The guy turns on his heels like a wounded prom queen. Lili says to Fiorella, "I didn't hear that? Can you say it louder?"

"Yes, Miss Lili." There's a pause. "...should I do that now?"

"That would be good, yeah."

"Okay. Mr. Mack passed. Then Miss Hillary."

"Are you saying 'passed' like dead?"

"—Like dead. Yes, Senorita. Miss Lili."

"—My father's dead?"

"Yes, Miss Lili."

"—And Hillary's dead, too?"

"Yes, Miss Lili."

"Okay, okay. Who the fuck is this?"

"It's me. Fiorella."

"No, no. This 'everybody's dead' shit. Who does that? What sort of sick person?"

There's two or three seconds of silence before Fiorella says, "—I-I'm so sorry, Miss Lili." This is the moment Lili realizes the woman is legit – it's the quiver in her voice, the sadness. Fiorella says, "I do not like making such a call, but I don't want you to find out from the policia. Or the TV."

"...what ... happened." Lili could barely hear her own voice.

"Miss Hillary was killed at Mr. Mack's funeral," Fiorella says. "People find her body in the woods. Her neck got cut."

"...Jesus." Lili shut her eyes. Her stomach is tight, a bitter taste coming up from the back of her throat. "—And my father?"

"A heart attack. But because of Miss Hillary, the policia think maybe this heart attack is murder, too."

Lili stays quiet.

"I think you should watch yourself," Fiorella says.

Tell me something I don't know, Lili thinks.

A BRIGHT BOY WHO HATED GYM

Madrid to Palencia
April 29th, Afternoon

HE'S GETTING USED to the trains. Grigor Bolian is leaning back in his seat, his tortoise shell Ray-Bans masking his face. Sunshine comes through the window and warms the skin. The train's rhythm has the motion of a cradle pushed by an angry mom.

Go to sleep, you little bastard, the clack-clack talking to him, over and over. *Go to sleep, you little bastard.* Then Grigor think, *C'mon, mom, get closer so I can puke on you.* He smiles to himself. The doctor has a good sense of humor.

"*Billete*, senior."

"...what?"

"—Ticket."

The old conductor takes the ticket and gives part of it back as a receipt. He does not look at Bolian. Bolian thinks the conductor doesn't look at him because it's a boring job and the man has been doing this boring job for thirty years and he probably goes home and gets drunk and plays with a loaded pistol.

"Have a fucking nice day," Bolian mutters. He is still leaning back. His eyes are closed behind the Ray-Bans.

Grigor's thinking about Ray and Hill, especially Hill. He liked killing Ray but he hated killing Hill. Ruined him for hours. He keeps thing about '96 and Kara Nissim's party in the Village, where he'd met her. So damn pretty

187

and fun then. And God the bitch could fuck. What a waist. Unbelievable. Why did she have to go and get all *Call of Duty* on him?

"—*Shit, just shit,*" The Commander whispering. Grigor doesn't have to open his eyes to know that no one's there. Oh he can smell the presidential cologne, perhaps its Armani. Who knows. All his imagination, anyway, but definitely presidential. Now The Commander says, *"The way some things turn out for us. A man can't allow some little sweetheart to wave a gun in our face, though, can we?"*

"No, sir," Grigor whispers back. "—He cannot. Or in this case, she cannot. She *definitely* cannot. I am all for protecting the ones you love. I'm all for people saying what's on their mind. This is what America is about, I understand that. But that shit has a shelf life, you know? Speak but do not disrespect, that's what I say."

"You have to keep the world in line."

"It's true," Grigor says, his voice close to a whisper. "Somebody fucks with you, you fuck them back and you fuck them back harder and better. Respect is a fragile thing.

Nobody *owes* you respect."

"—Amen, son," The Commander is overcome with pride. "You are one of those rare creatures who knows what is expected of him. Aman and *amen.*" Grigor can hear

The Commander's pride in each word.

He'd always thought Hill resembled his whore mother, anyway, her eyes, her hair, the way she moved. But he knew the difference between his mother and Hill. Hill would never let Uncle Revig put a dick in her. King of Syracuse dry cleaning. The fat bastard and the whore mother deserved each other.

"You're father was crying, wasn't he?" The

Commander says. *"—In the kitchen, crying like some bitch?"*

"I wouldn't call him 'some bitch,' exactly."

"Don't you get soft on me now," The Commander says, a sternness in his voice. *"Don't forget, we must always be honest with ourselves. Take that harsh look. That was the hallmark of my administration, you know."*

"My actions are my own." Grigor believes that's the truth.

He'd give Uncle Revig tea made from the mushroom *Gyromitra esculdenta.* The man was dead in six days but not before many hours of vomiting and diarrhea. Grigor had sat in the bedroom with him, even held his head during the vomiting.

Why not, what's family for?

"—Excellent. Spoken like a warrior." The Commander's sternness has shifted to something close to pleased. *"My judgment of you remains impeccable. I'm constantly amazed at my ability to spot the right individual for the right job."*

"I appreciate the confidence." Dr. Bolian likes to give credit where it's due.

"I feel such a pride in you." The Commander's voice has a slight quiver. *"You'll continue on, of course. You must conclude your business."*

"—Oh absolutely."

"Do not question why you do something." The Commander is at his best when he's giving his famous Life Lessons. *"You do a thing because it's the road you must go down. Do not lose yourself in Freudian crap. Mommy had tiny titties, that sort of thing. Let no history guide you, doctor. We make our own history every day."*

Right. None of that psychoanalytic crap for Grigor Bolian. No thank you, sir and/or madam. None of that crackpot Freud: mom made me do this; dad made me do that. How many kids with whack-job parents turn out just fine, hell, become our fine congressmen and women? A shit load, that's how many.

Grigor believes his classmates remember him as a bright boy who got As. He loved biology and hated gym. *Most kids hated gym, except the jocks*, he thinks. *Black kids and big goofy whites. Jesus, they loved gym.* Nobody but jocks and homos liked wearing white gym shorts. Grigor had escaped other regrettable acts besides killing his uncle. In his tenth year he developed an interest in fire. He liked setting traps for small animals in the field near his home, squirrels, field mice, the occasional raccoon. Grigor would light them up with kerosene and a kitchen match. They'd and twist and shriek and run across the open field. This was mostly a night time activity. Grigor recorded their behavior in his school composition book, such variables as the distance traveled before death, how many separate, distinct screams, the amount and degree of burned skin area, etcetera, etcetera. Even then the doctor had an interest in science.

SHOOT ME, ALREADY

THE CONVERSATION HASN'T changed in four days. Lili would like to go somewhere alone for awhile, anywhere – nothing permanent, just for awhile, just to find a place to scream. The same questions, day after day. Who is the person, or maybe *persons*, who killed her dad and Hillary? The other question is, who is Fiorella and is she really who she says she is, can she be trusted?

Lili Mack and Isaac are sitting on the stony edge of a four lock canal in Fromista. The canal is 126 miles long and took a century to build, what Lili's guide book says. Mostly barges use it to carry grain.

This morning is already humid and the clouds are dark.

"Can you trust her?" Isaac says, meaning Fiorella.

"She didn't have to call, right? Am I right?"

"—Sort of ruins the surprise."

"—Exactly."

Isaac drapes his arm about Lili's thin shoulders and says, "I'm sorry about your, dad. I can't imagine being that close to one of my parents"

"Let's not go there. I can't believe they're dead, daddy especially." Lili gives a quick, brief wave of her hand, erasing the subject before it begins. Then she goes on with it, anyway. "I woke up this morning thinking, shit, I'm a forty-two year old orphan. It's so bizarre. A person is never too old to be an orphan."

"Why kill the girlfriend, too? Why Hillary?" Isaac Stalin is looking down at the muddy green water of the canal. He drops a stone into the water and watches the circles spread. "Maybe he's got a thing for symmetry," Isaac says, answering his own question. He should've just taken the money and gone somewhere, Paris maybe. If this is the guy who's coming after us, why bother? You know what I mean? Why not just pocket the money and walk?"

"He likes it," Lili says.

"— Likes what?" He turns and looks at her.

"—Killing."

"Great. I feel so much better." Isaac's all about irony this morning.

"Daddy talked to me about it. *Him*, the guy." Every now and again Lili feels a drop of rain taps her bare arm. "Hillary used to know this guy, they dated or whatever. He liked talking about creepy shit after sex, how people kill each other. Most bizarre pillow talk ever – stories about unsolved murders, things he'd read about or heard on TV. He loves killing the way some people love sex and chocolate."

"Hillary said the chocolate thing?"

"—Yeah." Lili is patting away the dampness from the back of her neck with a wrinkled white handkerchief. "He had surgical instruments on one of his bedroom walls. Knives, saws, you know, antiques." Lili smiles. more to herself than to Isaac. "He knew how to put a girl in the mood."

"Hillary said that?"

"I said that. It's a joke."

"—Not funny."

"What do people say? 'You laugh to keep from crying,' something like that?" Lili stands, presses her fingertips to her lower spine. She looks at the horizon, where the water from the canal meets the darkening sky. "This guy is going to kill us. He probably won't stop 'til he does. That's the sort of asshole he is. It doesn't matter if we leave or stay.

That doesn't mean we're going to hang out and wait for it, either. Fuck that. I'm not sure what we're going to do, but we're certainly *not* waiting for it."

Isaac hesitates a moment; then, "...I-I want to apologize, Lili."

"—'bout what?" She has to think for a second or two, go from one set of feelings and thoughts to another – *Christmas night at the pool.* He's been talking a lot about that last few days, nothing apologetic, only talking.

He gets up from the edge of the canal. "I've been going over stuff, how to talk about it, that time when we were kids."

Yes, Christmas night at the pool.

"That was the worst, a nightmare," Isaac says. "What if something happens to us – to me, I mean – and I don't say anything. I could've accidentally killed you that night." His hands are pushed deep into his pockets. His shoulders twitch at the thought. He says, "You could've hit your head and drowned."

"God. You *are* apologizing."

"It was a stupid boy thing."

"—Which?" Lili sees a bewildered look cross his face. "—Pushing me into the pool, or coming back later and fucking me?" The fucking part had always bothered her as much as the pushing part.

"You thought the sex was stupid?"

"I thought you running away was stupid."

DR. DARK MATTER AND THE INVISIBLE MAN

Palencia
May 2nd, Late morning

NORMAN PEARLMAN IS seated on a white wood bench in the Parque del Flores. Yellow, red and pink roses cover the ground and the tall trellises. Fragrance and sunshine envelope him. Bees reflect the light and become tiny bits of gold. He thinks what he's feeling must be like what happens when you shoot vodka into your veins. He's drunk on it, the smell, the sun, the beauty, the whole heavenly thing. The park also has gray pebbled walkways. Clipped hedges surround bronze and marble statues.

Last night the stars told Dr. Norm to wait in Palencia.

"That makes no sense," he had whispered, the scientist who wanted reason but longed for magic. Was such a desire even possible? He was at his hotel window looking at the bright dots in the dark sky. "I can't just do nothing."

"The one you are waiting for is coming."

"The man in the photograph?" He'd thought that immediately.

"—Yes. Look here at our revelation," the stars said. Perhaps there *was* the shape of a man in the sky, an image in a connect-the-dots sort of way. Norm Pearlman wasn't a hundred percent sure. Then he heard, *"This man is not too tall and not too short. But he is a man who's just right enough to get the job done."*

"No one is talking to me." Dr. Norm said that both to himself and the night sky. Said it to the stars who were talking to him. *My imagination, I'm sure. Like mama's voice*, he thought. How foolish to engage the inanimate. Why explain reality to a disinterested universe? "I must get to Lili before this madman gets to her." Norm felt out of breath just saying it. He felt he was already running toward her. "—A motor bike. I saw a place that rents them right in town."

"No, you do not need to find her."

Dr. Norm remembered being at the hotel window and hearing the stars tell him that – forget finding Lili, that was what he'd heard – and he felt his anger heat up the sides of his neck. How could he listen to anything that told him to forget his bride? Okay, his *ex*-bride. But still. Wasn't that the whole purpose – to find her and keep her safe?

"—No, no, no. Find the doctor."

Could the stars be right?

Was it his job to question the eternal? He suspected, no, no it was not. Faith is about following the message with as few questions as possible. Sacrifice that son. Build that ark. Walk into that parted sea. Listen to that burning bush.

Or ...

Act. Like. Eve. After. The. Apple.

"—Find him and kill him," the stars said.

"Of course, yes," Norm gave another whisper looking out his hotel window, another murmur to the infinite. And reason was set aside. "I will be a silent hero," he said. "A man of stealth. Isn't that why I'm here? To find and kill the doctor?"

"You are a true visionary," the stars whispered back.

"I have been lead by the divine, haven't I?" he said, believing once again in the power of the stars.

"Do we ever disappoint?"

Dr. Norm thought for a moment but couldn't recall if

the stars had disappointed him or not. He'd been lead to lovely Spain, that was for sure. And hadn't the old woman at the Cathedral Santiago de Compostela given him a photograph of this evil doer, this snake among men?

Aren't events clarifying themselves?

"Why yes," he now says to himself. "Yes, they are, all is being revealed. I must believe. I must practice patience."

"*—Patience and trust.*"

"If not you, who can I believe? I *am* you, after all." Dr. Norm has thought about this many times. "Let me tell you what we know, those of us who watch you, who bare witness. We are made of you – everything of us is you – like the baby to the parent. And our job is to be your eyes, to think about us. We are witnesses. We watch that majestic, never ending part of you...of us."

"*—And we guide you.*"

He can barely see the bees in the sunlight but he can hear them. The buzz of tiny golden bees, how positively amazing. The roses in the Parque del Flores intoxicate – their fragrance, the stark beauty of color and form. He has been lead to paradise. Who better to do that than the stars, the guides of ships and kings?

"*Please listen now,*" the stars are saying. They're hidden by daylight yet always present. "*The man you seek is here. He's seated on one of the benchers. You must stay resolute. Do not be seduced by bees and flowers.*"

Right away Dr. Norm cups his hand above his brow and glances about the Parque del Flores. First he looks at the shadows the statues cast on the gray pebble walkways. The park isn't big, nothing a person could use for hiding. He removed the photo from the inside pocket of his linen sport coat. The girl he'd be able to spot in a heartbeat. The man isn't so easy. There's no hook – fat, thin, gray hair, brown hair, ugly, handsome, not a damn thing. Sort of brownish hair but that was years ago. He could be bald now. He could –

    — It's him, I know it. I can feel it.

    About fifteen yards to his right, Dr. Norm saw a man on one of the wood benches. He wore khaki pants, a blue dress shirt and … was it loafers? Yes, okay, *brown* loafers. The man could be mid-forties, maybe early fifties.

    The man looks up and stares at him. Norm Pearlman forgets to breathe. Then the man in the blue shirt and Khaki pants waves and smiles.

TROUBLE AT WOUNDED KNEE

Sahagun
Leon, Spain
May 2, Afternoon

"I THINK YOU'VE got an infection," Lili says. She has been using antibiotic cream on Isaac Stalin's right knee since April 13th – how many days? Thirty-one or two, something like that. *The cream isn't doing the job.* She's sure of it. Then Lili says, "You need a real antibiotic."

"—H-How do you know?"

"Look at the red area."

Each morning she'd mark the wounded area with a dot from her pen. One or two days would go by with no spreading. On the third or fourth day the inflamed area would get bigger – two days of hope followed by a day of reality.

"We need to get you a doctor," Lili tells him; sees a hint of relief sweep his face. She says, "Don't get too disappointed."

"—You think its serious?" Isaac wants to know, his relief becoming concern. "I mean like dying or losing my leg. Be serious with me."

The town of Sahagun is a mix of crumbling tan stone churches, thick green fields and cart-wide dirt paths for wagons and beat up trucks. Long, heavy clouds have come in from the east and drift under the sun and put rolling shadows over fields and trees and old abandoned churches.

"I don't think absolution is in the cards for us," Lili says.

"They should do it by the mile."

"—A third absolution, a half absolution? That sort of thing?" She's using a clean piece of gauze soaked in alcohol to wash the infected area on Isaac's knee. "An 'A' for effort?"

"Hey, we suffered," he says, wincing at the alcohol. "That's got to count for something. Why does it have to be all or nothing?"

"You mean like half a crucifixion?"

"You're finding me amusing again. I'm glad I entertain you.'

Lili kisses him, just a quickie on the lips. About halfway into it she realizes she truly *does* like this guy. She's actually concerned about his stupid knee. Who would have thought it. The Same guy who busted up her ear and changed her life – maybe for the worse, maybe for the better, the way she looks at that hideous long ago night depends on how the day is going.

"Let's see if we can hitch a ride to a bigger town," she says, bandaging Isaac's knee. She helps him stand. "We got to get you a good doc."

"—You're serious." Now he looks concerned.

"Hey, you'll be fine. No worrying, okay?"

"I'm not talking about me," Isaac says, bending his knee. He walks a tight circle then bends the knee a second time. "You're serious about giving this up – our hike away your sins walkathon."

"My sins are fairly pathetic," she says.

"—Sorry about everything."

"Maybe this is what we need to do."

Lili thinks about the message written on the wall of the Ermita de Nuestra Señora de la Peña.

hi Isaac hi Lili

you guys having fun?

A shift in plans isn't that bad an idea.

It took them forty or so minutes to flag down an old flatbed that had several wood crates filled with noisy chickens. The driver must have been in his late seventies, his face creased from too much sun and too many cigarettes. The old man told them he was going to Palencia. Lili's guide book gives the addresses of both pharmacies and physicians there. They climb aboard and huddle in the far corner of the flatbed and watch the chickens.

"—Diseased beasts," Isaac mutters.

"Don't be too hasty." Lili tries not to smile but can't help herself. She says, "We could fry up a couple of those little beauties."

"You find me endlessly amusing."

"What can I say? It's a sin that won't be cleansed."

The rhythm and bump of the flatbed bed is something hypnotic, something lazy. Lili leans her head on Isaac's chest. His arm goes around her.

"Maybe we can throw the guy off," she says. "Hide out in the hospital. Or get ourselves a real hotel room."

"...what guy?" Isaac's eyes are half-closed.

"—Never mind."

"You mean the guy that's going to kill us no matter what? That guy?"

"Get some sleep," she whispers.

AS SHE LIVES AND BREATHES, JESSIE COLE

Palencia
May2rd, Late-morning

THE WOMAN IS on the train and waiting at the Palencia station. She's going to Madrid to see her first bullfight. That's when the doctor comes into view, she can't believe it. Had he ever told her his name? Recalling anything to do with him is painful, even frightening.

Bolian, isn't it? Or maybe it's not the gentleman at all.

But, no, there's that little bald spot on the back of his head. And that walk, that I'm Letting You Visit My World walk – who does he think he's kidding? He's heading toward the escalator and she decides the bullfight can wait. She can't be afraid her entire life. Who can live that way?

What Jessie Cole wants to do now is give the doctor – *ha*, some doctor, what sort of doctor does what he did – a major piece of her mind.

The nurse at the Hospital Virgen del Camino in Pamplona said Jessie's heart had stopped twice and how lucky she was to still be around and kicking. The nurse told her that *Amanita ocreata* was the mushroom used in the tea.

"They called it *El Angel de la Muerte*," the nurse said. She probably saw Jessie Cole's expression go blank. The nurse translated, "—You know, The Angel of Death."

Who does such a horrid thing?

The hotel housekeeper had found her still tied to the

headboard of the bed. Unconscious. Vomit everywhere. Thank God for housekeepers.

Jessie's ex-hubby, Warren, had told her about men like Dr. Bolian. "Sure they seem nice," he'd said. "Men like that always seem nice, Jess. A rattlesnake *seems* nice. Just don't get too close, or pet the damn thing, that's my advice. Not that you're asking for my advice, that'll be the day. Can't tell you a damn thing, never could."

She leaves the train, pulling her wheeled carry-on behind her. Feeling like shit too, a person doesn't get over what Jessie has gone through in a week or two – symptoms like to linger, the cramps, the loose bowels, the skipping beats of her heart. Thank God she didn't get hepatitis.

Don't let that bastard getaway.

She has a pistol in her travel bag, a derringer. Certain people think derringers are the Little Girl of pistols. These people are morons. Usually men. This one is a double barrel derringer, the black on black Cobra, used a .38. Her ex had given it to her three or four Christmases for their break up.

"You damn sure can kill someone with *this* derringer," her ex had said. He'd laughed and shook his head at the thought. Holiday eggnog had turned the day toasty and amusing. Her ex had said, "—A .38 isn't a .22, babydoll. I could'da got you a .22, but, shit, why not have a fighting chance. Am I right? You *know* I'm right. Get a .22 and the asshole you shoot is making deals with the lord. 'Let me live and I'll go to church and stop fucking my sister.' Unbelievable what folks do. But you get a .38 and those bastards are just dead. There's no praying. There's no nothing."

"—Very pretty," she had said about the derringer, the first words that came to mind when she unwrapped it. It *was* pretty – sort of dark and mysterious and cute all at once. "I have no idea what to do with this, you know."

"That's why God invented husbands."

Jessie Cole is remembering the derringer conversation with her ex as she takes the escalator up to ground level, hoping she hasn't lost Dr. Bolian. The late morning sunlight reflects off the sidewalk and the hoods of passing vehicles on the Calle Gil de Fuentes.

Where did you go, Doctor? Jessie's hand is already grasping the small pistol in her leather handbag. She doesn't bring it into the open but she wants to know where it is and how fast she can get to it.

C'mon. c'mon, I know you're here. I know it. People don't just disappear when they hit sunlight. Where are you, you creepy bastard?

It's the walk that gives him away, that ever-so-slight strut. He can hid everything but that. What would you call it – his arrogance, his condescending good will? The man likes to smile at passersby, a smile to this one, a smile to that one. He's a few yards ahead of her and crossing the street now, heading toward a park with its big shade trees and its red, yellow and pink flowers.

Roses, she thinks. *How lovely are the roses.*

Jessie remembers her last minutes with him at the Hotel de Peregrino. She'd been naked, her wrists tied to the wrought iron headboard with her own silk scarves. Through the closed door, Dr. Bolian told the bellhop to leave the cart in the hallway. The doctor had slipped on his blue gabardine pants and a white sleeveless undershirt. When Bolian rolled the cart into the room, what Jessie Cole saw first was a dark red rose in a glass.

Roses, she thinks again. *How lovely are the roses.*

Right away she knew the tea wasn't good. It tasted odd to her, a bitter, leathery taste, like no tea she'd ever known. Jessie had watched him take out a tiny envelope and pour the tannish-white contents into the cup of hot water.

"—But that rose was beautiful," she whispers to herself. "I can see it so very clearly, the most beautiful rose ever."

Dr. Bolian is halfway across the street – five, six yards in front of her – heading toward the park. The former Mrs. Cole doesn't care about what is proper and what is not, forget the social graces. In the middle of the sunlit morning, on the busy Calle Gil de Fuentes, Jessie fires both shots at the doctor. One shot connects and he grabs his upper left arm, almost losing his balance.

THE SORT OF NEWLYWEDS

Hospital Santos de Palencia
May 2nd, Early evening

"WE'LL KEEP HIM overnight," Miguel Espino says to Lili. He's tall and skinny and has delicate, manicured fingers and a skimpy hairline. But he could do commercials with those hands, that's what she thinks. Miguel is six months from completing his medical residency. He says, "We'll start an antibiotic. Ampicillin, probably." And to Isaac, "—No long walks for awhile, okay? Keep it to a little shopping. Maybe walk to a restaurant. " The man speaks terrific English; she thinks that, too. Dr. Espino turns back to Lili, "Are you the wife, senora?"

"Yeah, she's the wife," Isaac says. They are downstairs in Emergency. Isaac is sitting on a gurney, shorts off, wearing white jockeys. His right knee has been washed and dressed, fresh gauze and adhesive.

"—Sure, the wife." Lili gives Isaac Stalin a WTF look.

"—*Newlyweds*," Isaac tells the doc, more emphatically this time. Then he says, "You think she can stay with me in the room? A comfortable chair, I mean. Perhaps a blanket? We hate being apart, you know how it is."

"I wish I did," Dr. Espino says.

"I doubt you'll have trouble," Lili says. A little flirty.

"— How very kind." The doctor's starting to get flirty, too.

Isaac has the look of the odd guy out. A fucking love

fest, what Lili imagines him thinking. She says to the doc, "So we can leave tomorrow?"

"Let's get a couple of doses in him," the doc says.

"Hey, I'm the patient here." Isaac is sounding pissed but controlled. "How 'bout you talk to me."

A startled look goes over Dr. Espino's face, less than a second. "Of course, Mr. Stalin. It's been a long day, no offence."

There are four ceiling fans in Emergency, not a big room, not a little one, either. The walls are gray and the floor is white and black checked marble. Two of the windows are open and the breeze going through the room is cool and damp.

You're jealous. Lili can't believe it. Then she considers Isaac's attitude and *can* believe it. *You love a woman whose father wanted you dead. Maybe I wanted you dead, too. I'm sure that's crossed your mind. I'm guessing you've given that idea a lot of consideration.*

It doesn't matter how many times they save each other. The damage he did to her and the contract her father put out on him is in The Book. It's history. Lili gets it. You can't rewrite The Book. You can't erase The Book. The Book is bomb proof and resistant to time and climate and the turning of the earth.

You can't even drone the bitch.

People will say, "Remember when Isaac Stalin pushed Lili Mack into the pool and busted her ear and basically fucked up her life? Remember when Lili's dad, Raymond, put a contract out on Isaac?"

"Wow. Those were the days," others will say.

Fun times.

When Dr. Espino leaves and they are alone, Lili tells Mr. Pouty Boy, "Try not to get all weird and grumpy on me, okay?" She says this under her breath. Isaac is about to object and she puts an index finger to his lips. "—*Shhh,* no, no. Just be a good guy. I just saved you from gangrene, or whatever. So be appreciative."

Isaac holds up the flat of his hand and nods. "You're right, I apologize. When you're right, you're right."

"At least our friend isn't looking for us here," she says.

"—Currently."

"Fine, yeah. *Currently*." Isaac's right, though. She'll give him that much. No getting too confident in a situation. "I'm not about to say we're home free, believe me. Who knows when that asshole will show himself."

"There's no time limit, you know?" Isaac is looking down at the new bandage on his knee. "We'll be looking for this guy our entire lives. We can never relax, some fucking life. We'll never know if he's given up or not."

"He's done some good," she whispers and touches his face with the palm of her hand. "You know, I don't think this trip was a waste, Isaac. Don't get me wrong, I still think you're sort of a pain in the ass. But part of you is I dunno – en*dear*ing. The way you worry about things. How you've looked after me."

"Let me say, I still feel like shit. Probably always will." Isaac eases himself from the gurney. He bends his leg and winces. "I'm talking about what I did that night. When we were kids, I mean. If I could take it back I would, Lili, but you know how that is. 'If wishes were horses, beggars would ride.' What can a person do?" He hesitates then leans toward her and kisses her. The suddenness of it startles Lili but his lips are warm and she relaxes and kisses him back. He says, "I'm glad we did everything –you finding me, the trip, the whole deal."

"You can thank my father." Lili shuts her eyes, a second, two. When she opens

them, her vision is blurry and she feels her tears. "...you could thank him, if he was, you know, around. Before this trip, I'd of gone along with pretty much anything daddy said. Girls and their daddies, right? Particularly mine. But I've always been happy with my life. I like teaching. I like my kids – my students. I *love* my kids. Maybe it takes the great Raymond Mack dying to say no to him."

THE REALITIES OF DRS. GRIGOR AND NORM

In an Ambulance
May 2ⁿᵈ, Early evening

THEY'RE HEADING toward Hospital Santos de Palencia. Dr. Norm is in the back of the ambulance with Dr. Bolian. The siren has that European air raid sound, a breathing, in and out, in and out.

"You can't direct Spanish men," Grigor Bolian mutters. One of the two shots had missed, the other had gone into the bicep of his left arm. He's laying on a collapsed gurney and hooked to a monitor for vitals, a clear plastic oxygen tube clipped between his nostrils, his arm temporarily bandaged. "I told the driver, 'No, siren.' Didn't you hear me say no siren? I thought I was pretty clear."

"You were very clear," Dr. Norm says.

"—Sounds like the fucking Nazis are coming. I can't believe that piece of shit shot me."

"What piece of shit?"

"—Not that she didn't have a reasonable grudge," Grigor says.

"She a girlfriend?"

"I should've killed her awhile back."

"—So a girlfriend?"

Grigor stares at Dr. Norm. "Do men do shit like this?" He doesn't wait for an answer. "No, never. It's always women with tiny pistols."

"How did you know it was tiny?"

"I *looked*, you dope."

"Well tiny pistols can kill people, too." Norm Pearlman pauses; realizes he may have said the wrong thing and goes in another direction, "I'm not saying you're dying, Grigor. Hey, I'm not a physician. I'm a universe guy. Big Bang. Inflation. Andromeda colliding with the Milky Way. What do I know, right?"

The back of the ambulance smells of urine and lavender disinfectant, and there is hardly enough room for one person.

Dr. Norm cannot quit thinking about last night and his newest epiphany. Last night he'd looked up at the stars and saw the scenario that is now revealing itself – his meeting in the park with Grigor Bolian, the man's pistol wound, their ride in this very ambulance to the Hospital Santos de Palencia.

My dear God, I am a prophet, Dr. Norm thinks. He has his Glock 17 in a holster under beneath his gray khaki sport coat. Clean. No shot fired. *I'm like a Nostradamus. Like Abraham and Solomon. A man born of the stars – me, Norman Pearlman.* He tries to remember the end of his revelation but it has escaped him.

It's all so déjà vu.

"Let me ask you a question," Dr. Norm says to Bolian.

"Can't you see I'm wounded?"

Norman wishes he could fathom this man, this potential cry baby. "Answering a question won't make you more wounded, okay?"

"Have *you* ever been shot?"

"—actually ... yes." *Are you really going to tell him?* Is shooting yourself with a pistol the same as having someone else shoot you? Dr. Norm decides, *why yes, yes it is. Only more stupid.* He says, "I shot myself."

"—You did what?" Already there is a bit of a smile.

"—In an extremity. However, in my defense, I was

very young and had no idea what I was doing. Also, I was emotionally distraught."

Grigor Bolian now has a big smile. Dr. Norm feels good about that. A happy attitude is always therapeutic.

Norm says, "After my father got back from military service, he was a changed person and he'd beat my mother for any reason, for *no* reason. It didn't matter. They'd mostly fight at night but I could hear them from my bedroom. Lots of yelling and crying. My father thought my mother was cheating on him. Or that she was too bossy. Or that she didn't listen to him when he told her to do this or that. The man had an ever changing list and almost anything she did could get him upset."

"Did you shoot him, eventually?" Grigor wants to know.

"No, my first and last time with a gun," Dr. Norm says. He is sitting on a small metal seat at the foot of the gurney. "—Until you. I took lessons from the father of one of my students. Another retired military person. There's a lot to it – shooting a gun. Technically, of course. But there's a whole psychological thing, too."

"You learned to shoot because of me? I'm flattered."

"I didn't do it to flatter you," Norm says. "I did it to kill you."

Grigor is still relaxed and smiling. "What's the psychological part?"

"—To feel okay about it."

"—Shooting somebody?"

"—Shooting *you*." Norms thinks it's time to discuss realities. "Look, let's talk about the situation."

"What situation is that?" The guy won't stop being amused.

"Raymond Mack is dead," Dr. Norm says. "I think you know that. That means nobody is coming for your 75k. No matter what you do – shoot or don't shoot the Stalin asshole – the money is in your account. I will also let you keep my fee – that's 85K to wound but not kill the asshole – and you don't have to lift a finger. You don't have to do anything to anyone and you get to keep the whole 160 thousand. Think about it. You walk away with 160K and don't you don't do shit. What do you say?"

Grigor shuts his eyes. "Oh c'mon, sport," he whispers. "What fun would that be?"

THE ASSASSIN'S ASSASSIN

Palencia, Calle Gil de Fuentes
May 2nd, Early evening

SHE'D NEVER SEEN such a small ambulance. Did only people under five feet get sick in Palencia? Jessie Cole had watched the ambulance pass her on the Calle Gil de Fuentes. This happened twenty or so minutes after she fired two shots at Grigor Bolian and saw him run into the park across the street. Hiding among the roses and the bees, most probably.

That's where the ambulance had gone to pick his ass up.

Big man when a woman is tied to the bed, she's thinking. *Not so fucking big now, are we, lover?*

The derringer had made a louder noise than she'd remembered. Frightened her, actually. Jessie's ex-hubby, Warren, would've found her whole freak out far too typical and way too funny.

"Get it the fuck together, girl," she imagined him saying. Then a dramatic sigh and his usual, "—*Women,* what can you do?" Followed by, " I'm surprised you didn't close your eyes when you shot the man."

No one had noticed the shots on Calle Gil de Fuentes, or no one she'd seen. The traffic had continued to creep along, the occasional horn, the occasional tires coming to a quick stop. Maybe folks thought the gunshot had been the backfire of an old vehicle, a truck, a car, a bus. Some weary, mechanical fart.

Scared the shit out of Jessie, though.

Immediately she'd retreated into the shaded alley between a tan brick apartment building on one side and a poultry shop on the other, the shop advertising geese, ducks and chickens freshly slaughtered on the premises, a blue and yellow neon sign – *aves de corral sacrificadas en las instalaciones.* Behind her are four stinky metal garbage cans filled with rotted bird carcasses.

Her ex would've said, *"—My wife, a fugitive from justice."*

"Shut up, Warren," she whispers.

There is nobody there. Jessie knows that but looks behind her anyway. Just in case. Maybe it's Warren; maybe it's people watching her talk to herself. She can't decide what's worse – being nuts or being humiliated.

You need to chill the You-Know-What out, okay? she thinks. *Everybody talks to themselves. People imagine stuff, that's how we are. Of course, a few people imagine shit a lot more than others.*

She's looking down at her navy blue carry-on with the pop up handle, the sort pilots and flight attendants use. Perhaps people would see her as an attendant crazed by the possibility of terrorism.

This is when she looks across the street and sees the ambulance leaving the park with its lights twirling, with its siren at full volume. You'd have thought the prime minister of Spain or a TV celebrity had been shot.

Her first thought is to go back to the train station and get out of Palencia. Doesn't matter where, just out. Anywhere. She could take one of those ferry boats and go to Morocco. Tangier. What's wrong with living out her last years in Tangier? Get a little apartment. Go shopping. Sip tea, smoke a little hash. *I could drink tea and watch the ocean.* Then she thinks, *Oh, God, toss the pistol. Do what people do in the movies, wipe it with a handkerchief, remove your fingerprints. Afterward, you toss the pistol in a lake or the Castilla Canal. Yes, that's it, the canal.* But Jessie doesn't know where the canal is, exactly, and she doesn't want to walk around with a murder weapon in her handbag. *Okay, maybe not a murder weapon. Let's not get dramatic. The doctor is obviously still alive. You don't waist a siren on a dead person.*

What would her ex do? Warren, the podiatrist. You can always tell an insecure person by the number of certificates on the wall. Jessie has learned this by watching her ex wheel and deal in the world of lower extremities. Warren had two complete walls covered with certificates. Mr. Too Important for His Clothes. One certificate was for giving free fungal examines to the members at the Sacramento Chamber of Commerce.

Wait a damn minute.

Jessie has started to pace back and forth in the alley and dragging her wheeled carry-on behind her. One of the little wheels is squeaking. *Walk, walk; squeak, squeak,* how can she decide shit with all that noise. Lord, lord. She actually shushes the wheels of the carry-on. *Really? What the fuck, get it together. And one of the first rules of getting it together is not to have arguments with inanimate objects.*

Reasonable advice.

Jessie Cole calmed herself by doing her Tai Chi breathing. Usually she'd move her arms and legs in slow and graceful motions as she breathed but not today. Today she decides thinking not motion is paramount. *Breath in; breath out.* Today she must dig into the pit of her soul and search the very stuff of her *raison d'etre*, so-to- speak. This is when she says to herself, "You're job is not to get rid of the murder weapon until it *becomes* a murder weapon."

THE NEW PATIENT

Hospital Santos de Palencia
May 2nd, Night

ISAAC FEELS LIKE he's been asleep forever. His digital watch reads 1:42 AM.

Lili Mack is sleeping in the chair next to his bed, a white cotton blanket about her legs. The windows are open and the fans above them turn slow and make a breeze and blow about the cool, damp air.

You look beautiful, he thinks, staring at Lili in the shadow and the moonlight. He loves watching her sleep. He knows this could be seen as semi-creepy but he likes what he likes. Her mouth is open slightly, though the woman isn't snoring. Isaac can't recall a time when she made a noise that disturbed his sleep. Lili is the quietest sleeper he's ever known and more than once Isaac has leaned over and listened to see if she were alive or dead.

Now he glances toward the other side of Emergency. There are a row of beds on both sides of the room, the nurses station in the middle of it all and lighted with desk lamps. Everything else is left to the moonlight. Isaac remembers an empty bed across from him but the bed isn't empty anymore. A new patient has arrived. Next to the bed is someone in a chair – a man, Isaac believes, an obese man. The man's hands are folded and resting on his stomach. He reminds Isaac of the actor Sidney Greenstreet from *The Maltese Falcon* – greatest movie ever – a movie written, directed and acted by gods.

Who the fuck are you? Isaac thinks. *Who's your friend in the bed?* Isaac doesn't want new people entering his life, new little mysteries, not in his present circumstance.

Suppose he has to defend himself? Suppose he and Lili have to flee? He cannot run on his damn leg right now. He has no weapon to defend himself, to defend Lili. *What the hell am I supposed to do?* It would be different if he were a fighter, somebody who knew how to handle situations. *I'm a cello player, for godsake. I'm not the person you call for this type of thing.*

Isaac remembers one of his father-son talks.

"You were always a sickly child." William Stalin started most talks with his son by telling Isaac who was strong and who was not. This time they were in the kitchen having Sunday morning waffles. Sunlight glittered off the brushed metal stove and the double door refrigerator.

"Boy Time," Isaac's mom, Ramona, called it; also, her morning to sleep-in.

William. was saying, "Our constitutions aren't our fault. This is the fate of genes. There were many sickly types on your mother's side."

"Leave her alone." Isaac hated how his father did that – all the shitty comments, the man's voice soft, almost gentle when he said them, a condescending, "poor thing, God bless her" attitude.

"Why say terrible things?"

Why did his mother suffer through these attacks, this on going humiliation? Has she become desensitized to it? Does she believe William Stalin 's propaganda and feel lucky he has enough humanity to overlook her obvious flaws?

How fortunate to marry this dear insightful man. Is this what she tells herself?

Knowing his mom, Isaac wouldn't be surprised if she included the asshole in her daily prayers. *May my beloved husband always care enough to guide me through this harsh world.*

"—Don't go getting me wrong," his father is saying.

"I'm not the sort who'd suggest your mom is responsible for your current condition."

"I don't have a condition."

"—*But* genetics *are* genetics, Isaac. Facts are facts, that's all I'm saying." His father was buttering his waffle as he talked. "You're designed for a far more sensitive life. No rough and tumble for you, sport."

Isaac believed William used the nickname "sport" in an ironic way, as if the man thought his son was anything but a sport – his boy, his uncomfortable joke. Isaac couldn't recall a time when he'd done well enough to see pride in his father's eyes.

"I'm not what you think I am. I've never been that boy." Isaac had watched the butter on his father's waffle melt and slide off its edges. "You look at me and talk about me like I'm another boy, somebody I don't know. Maybe that's the boy you want."

"That's the boy I have," William said, looking at him now, his serious, Don't Get Smart With Me face. "People are given what they are given – genes, a weak parent, a bad attitude, name your misfortune. It's up to us to overcome our bad deals. Do you understand what I'm telling you?"

Silence.

"I'm talking to you, Bill."

"What do want me to say?" The boy forever felt trapped by these father-son talks. He didn't want to answer; never wanted to answer. He didn't want to give a legitimacy to the old man's hustle. He didn't like being dragged into all that angry molasses. That day Isaac said, "You sound like a crazy person."

"—Ex*cuse* me?"

Isaac had stayed quiet, no apology, no nothing. He waited for William to release fire and piss from his godly perch – Zeus with raging, deadly bolts – but his father did nothing, not a damn thing. The old man didn't look at him. He poured syrup on his waffles. He cut the waffles in neat squares and began eating one square at a time.

The asshole had folded.

You reach a point where risking it all is what you do. This is what Isaac Stalin is thinking now – here in the Hospital Santos de Palencia, here in Emergency. He looks across the moonlit room at the big man in the chair and whoever is in the bed next to him.

There is a point where choices leave you. Risk is simply the next step.

LONG TIME NO SEE

WHEN LILI WAKES, she has no idea where she is, not at first. It takes a second, two before she remembers.

... hospital ... okay, right.

It's the disinfectant smell, the uncomfortable plastic chair – how could she forget? She's about to turn and ask Isaac how he's feeling but she sees a familiar person on the other side of the room. The man's looking at her, too – oh *my God* – a big, dumb face disguises Dr. Norm, Child of the Universe.

Norman Pearlman waves to her.

WTF. She waves back.

What are you doing here? Lili thinks, as if she didn't know. *The constellations have been chatting it up, haven't they?* She squints her eyes, cupping the palm of her hand above her brow, shading what? Starlight? It's definitely him. *But who are you with? Who's that lump in the bed beside you?*

Lili already has an idea about that one, too.

Norm walks over to her – very close to a tip-toe – and puts an index finger to his lips. "Keep quiet," he whispers. "Don't be mad. And don't wake the guy." He nods toward the other side of the room and the lump in the bed.

"That's him, isn't it?" She's whispering, too. "What's-his-name – Bolian?"

"I've got it under control."

Don't kid yourself, Lili thinks. *How can somebody so smart be so dumb?* She's sure controlling Bolian isn't what people do.

"Still no faith, huh?"

"Fine. You have a plan?"

Dr. Norm unbuttons his gray khaki sport coat and

shows Lili a glimpse of the holstered pistol, his Glock 17. "—The man with the plan."

"You going to shoot him?" Her voice rises a decibel. She brings it down to a hushed tone. "That's your plan – *shooting* him?"

Isaac sits up in the bed. Lili snaps her fingers to get his attention and makes a *shhh* sound. He whispers, "Who's the cretin?"

Lili does introductions.

"That's your *ex*?" Isaac gives her a Are You Kidding Me look.

Dr. Norm isn't thrilled either. "You're choices always surprise me."

"Can we do this later?"

Lili is looking at the other side of the room. The lump in the bed hasn't moved. *This little meeting wouldn't have happened in Madrid.* She's sure of it. Medical facilities are everywhere in Madrid, hospitals, clinics. you name it. Nobody bumps into anybody in Madrid. Raymond used to tell her how each bullfighting arena had at least two hospitals within a three block range.

"—Sixty medical facilities in that town," he'd said. "Madrid has a hospital in every neighborhood."

Palencia is a small town, people pass through to get to some place else. Lili's pretty sure Palencia's got one, maybe two hospitals. If you didn't want to meet up with people you've been avoiding, a person would have to eat right, exercise and stay away from firearms.

"What're we now?' Isaac's keeping his voice down. "—The three musketeers, or some shit?" He sounds like the musketeer thing is a betrayal.

Lili ignores him. Says to the ex, "I know you, Norman. You don't go around killing people, even men like Bolian. That's not you." She pauses, studying his face, not a speck of info there, nothing. Then she says, "Did you even have a plan?"

"—Talk to him," Norm says, a nervous shrug. "Nothing earth shaking, no great scheme. I just thought we could talk. You know, two sensible guys."

"Ahh. women of science."

"Something like that, yeah."

"How's that working for you?" Isaac gives a little snort.

Dr. Norm is looking down at his worn Nikes. Lili remembers this outfit, the Nikes, the sport coat, the jeans. That's all the man has ever worn.

"He could walk away with a lot of money," Norm says, talking about Bolian. "—Thousands. Won't have to do a thing, everybody wins. I thought he'd be able to see that. So simple, so obvious. We could reach a what-have-you, an understanding."

"You did talk to him?"

"—In the park, I did. In the ambulance, too. We talked about it a couple of times. Or I talked about it. He listened."

"I bet he's a great listener." Isaac says.

Dr. Norm shoots him a look. "Hey, I'm *not* naïve. This asshole murdered my lawyer, my friend. Cut his throat, I'm sure it was him." And to Lili, "You remember Jake – all bones and this really pale skin? He came over the house a couple of times?"

"—Cut his throat?" Lili says, ignoring the memory lane part.

"Jake met Bolian in Medina. I sent him there to offer the guy a deal; to stop him from going after you two."

"What 'you two' are we discussing?" Isaac says.

"—As in you and Lili."

Lili Mack is looking across the room, its long shadows, its stretches of silver light. She feels her heartbeat heavy at the sides of her neck. She can't get her breath.

The lump in the bed isn't there, anymore.

THE GETAWAY

THE CAB DRIVER parks his cab next to the curb on Calle Gil de Fuentes. He gets out, shuts the door and simply walks off.

"Hey!" Jessie can't believe this shit. The ambulance coming out of the park had *Hospital Santos de Palencia* on its side, and she knows finishing what she started is not debatable. Dr. Bolian isn't the sort of man who's going to let her grow fat and old. And Jessie yells, "Mister! *Senor!*"

What driver stops his cab and goes for a stroll?

"—En un momento, senorita," the cabbie says.

"Hey!"

"—En un momento." He's not turning around to look at her.

"*Hey!*" Jessie leans her head out the back window. The night is warm and the rain is very light and she can feel tiny cool drops on her face. "Hey, bud! Hey, damn it! Don't you 'en un momento' me, you bastard. Get *back* here."

The cabbie begins talking to a short, beefy woman in a tight red dress that goes mid-thigh. The woman's hair is black, curled. She's wearing gold hoop ear-rings and gold and silver bracelets.

The cabbie offers her one of his small thin cigars and they start smoking. He's a forty-ish guy with long sideburns and one of those golfer caps. His Hawaiian shirt has palm trees on it along with a blue sky and clouds. He's wearing Bermuda shorts and has no hair on his bony tan legs.

Son of a bitch. Jessie wishes she knew the Spanish

227

word for "emergency" or for "Get your ass back in the car." Something. She'd taken Spanish in high school but that was long ago and nowadays she couldn't remember her panty size without looking at the damn label.

Jessie has started digging through her leather handbag, muttering whatever curse words came to her mind. She finds her purse and pulls out two balled up fives and a ten. She flattens the bills on the backseat then starts waving them out the window.

"Hey! *Hey*, cabbie!" *What the hell is money in Spanish?* Jessie thinks. Then she actually remembers, "— Dinero! *Mucho* Dinero!"

Nothing.

This is when Jessie Cole opens the cab door and leaves the backseat. The cab is a bright red and yellow, 1963 Plymouth Fury. She now sits herself in the front seat on the driver's side, shuts the door and starts the engine.

When the car backfires, the fat woman in the red dress squeals and covers her ears. The cabbie flicks away his half-smoked cigar and begins running toward his cab He's shaking his fist and yelling some angry Spanish shit.

Jessie sticks her hand out the window, gives him the finger and steps hard on the gas pedal. The Plymouth jerks twice – a quick stop-start, stop-start. This pisses her off. She'd like to have one cool exit in her life before she dies. Jessie glances in the rearview mirror and sees the cabbie throwing his golfer's cap on the street, stomping it once with his foot.

Okay, that's pretty good.

Warren, her ex, should be here. He would give her one of his Thumb's Up. He was like the third Siskel and Ebert. You know, like Murray the K was the fifth Beatle.

"You're getting' me hot, baby," he'd have said, watching the cabbie stomp his hat. "—A little wood growing in the fire." That was one of his expressions. "A little wood growing in the fire." Like the "fire of our love," that sort of fire. He'd have said, "How 'bout you let me drive. C'mon. You can sit on my lap." That's where he would give her a wink. "We can be the Bonne and Clyde of Palencia – stealing cabs, humping in the front seat."

Oh, Warren, she thinks. *You're some card.*

Maybe he would also warn her. "Don't do this thing, Jess. The boy don't play – he *likes* killing, the way people like golf or watching football on TV."

"I can handle myself," she imagines telling him.

"I'm not saying you can't. Who's saying that?"

"—You're *inferring* it."

"Okay, okay. What the fuck ever."

He was a protector, though – *her* protector, used to be, anyway – or faked it damn good. She never knew with him. Jessie once saw him with his hand on Heather Rosenthal's twenty-eight year old ass at the neighborhood July 4th BBQ. Just resting it there like it was a cot. They were talking movie trivia – how many movie stars are homos and lesbians, that type of shit. Name eight current movie stars who are Scientologists. Jessie could only think of three.

"If you kill Bolian, the cops will find you."

"Thank you for loving me, Warren"

"Jess, don't do this." His voice sounds very distant.

She didn't answer him.

LONG TIME NO SEE
PART 2

Hospital Santos de Palencia
May 2nd, Night

"IF YOU WERE going to kill him, you'd have done it by now," Isaac Stalin says, waiting for Dr. Norm to give him the Glock. Isaac's holding out his hand, palm up. "It's *my* fight, Norm, not yours – mine ... and Lili's." The three of them have been whispering about who should use the pistol for three or four minutes. Isaac says, "But this is my problem, mainly. You know it's true. The contract – or whatever it was or *is* – has to do with Yours Truly."

The Emergency room is still dark with breaks of moonlight. In the center of the room is a partitioned area that has desks and florescent lamps. Three nurses occupy the desks, two of them are men.

"You've got a bad leg," Lili says to Stalin. "I should have the gun."

"—Not in this lifetime, kiddo." Isaac takes the Glock from Dr. Norm. "The guy's after me, that's what he was hired to do. What sort of a person would I be if I let you or Dr. Universe here fight my little war?"

"He right," Norm says to Lili. His shoulders droop ever-so-slightly. "I'm kidding myself. It's embarrassing to say but I-I had a bunch of opportunities to kill Bolian and I didn't – couldn't, just *couldn't* – do it." The big man points to the pistol in Isaac's hand. "The safety's off – just point and shoot."

"I *know* what to do." Too defensive, perhaps. He looks

231

at Lili and rubs her back, a quick and gentle motion, with the flat of his hand. "I do, you know."

Lili Mack watches Isaac limp into the darkness, the pistol raised, arms stiff. *I can't let him do this by himself*, she thinks. Lili hears the on-going muted chatter from the staff behind the partitions in the center of the room. There is an occasional laugh or a word clearly said.

"I'm going to follow him," Lili says to Norm.

"I'd like you to stay here with me. I know I can't stop you. It's not my place to do that, anyway." Dr. Norm's glazing down at his beat up Nikes. "If you think about it, what can you do? What's the point? It's not like you have an extra weapon, Lili. Or you know marshal arts. What can you do, for godsake?"

"I dunno. Be an extra pair of eyes."

"Bolian may not even be in the room," Norman Pearlman says. "He's capable of God only knows. He could be halfway to the train station by now."

"Then neither one of us will get hurt."

She could tell Norm didn't want to give up. He says, "Isn't Isaac the one who pushed you in the pool? Did you forget that – how self-absorbed he is? How out for himself? He didn't care about you then. Didn't care whether you lived or died that night. Probably would've preferred you dead. Why think he cares about you now?"

"Things change, Norm. Everything has a shelf-life."

"... so you say." Almost inaudible.

"So I do," Lili says.

She'd forgotten about his "tone," his whatever you'd call it, that helpless, What

Can You Do With This Child tone – a bad attitude from their long ago lives. It always left her feeling even more petulant, more determined to do what he didn't want her to do.

"You've never been able to listen to reason," he says.

"Who's reasoning?"

"You know what I mean."

"No, I don't get you at all." Lili's whisper is becoming sharp. "I forgot about you, how you act. We didn't have a marriage, Norm, we had teachable moments. We had the professor and the wife who sat in the front row."

"This isn't the place —"

"No, no, we're *not* doing that shit, Norman. It's not your place to tell me what's right and wrong. See that's *your* problem — Dr. Norm and his traveling classroom. Don't tell me *anything*. Like you know. That's what you do, exactly — instruct. And with the nicest manners. I'd forgotten, but you've always been that way."

Norm tries to place his hand on her shoulder. She shakes it away.

"God, why am I not surprised?" she says. "This is like the old days. I'd disagree with you and you'd think I was crazy. Dear, crazy Lili. Never content, never thinking it through, never listening to anyone."

Lili cups her hand above her brow again, peering into the shadows and the light from the moon, trying to spot Isaac. *Where are you? C'mon, Isaac boy, give me a break. Show yourself.* He isn't there, no limping silhouette going between the rows of beds, the snores and groans of new patients, nothing.

"At least let me call the police," Norm says.

"Yes. Okay, fine. Do that, please."

Then Lili Mack disappears into the darkness of the room.

WAITING ON STALIN

THIS IS TOO easy, what Grigor's thinking. He's watching the fag cello player wandering about the Emergency room, all hunched and limping along, arms outstretched, holding a pistol with both hands. A Glock, maybe. Less than a minute ago a male nurse brought medication to a patient. The fag crouched behind one of the beds like cops and crooks do on TV.

Come here, kitty-kitty – you and your big gun.

Grigor can see his opponent's fear. Stalin is crouching too low to the ground, his abrupt sweeping motions are erratic, the weapon dipping and correcting. There's also his limp, the bandaged knee, such a condition adds to a person's jitters – the wounded cello player on the prowl, his reaction time handicapped.

It's amazing he can stand, Bolian thinks. *Good for you, faggot.*

In less than thirty seconds Isaac Stalin will be an easy grab. That option has it's good and not so good points. A possible stress-free take down leads the list of good points, but bad points abound. Because of his unsteadiness, Stalin could fall in an unexpected way with a loaded gun. There is no workable plan for a loaded firearm falling to earth except to not go there.

— Twenty-five seconds.

Here's another problem. Let the gun go off and there would be enough cops for a shirts vs. skins soccer game. That's never a good thing. Grigor Bolian isn't sure of the terrain, either. What's the fastest path out? Can they secure the building from a central location; that is, can they do a lockdown? How soon before the staff finds Mr. Cello laying on the floor with a broken neck?

— Nineteen seconds.

Then there's the bitch who shot him.

What the hell is her name? he thinks. *Jessie Something. If you shoot a man in daylight on a busy street and see him run away, are you the sort of person who doesn't give up? Do you follow him? Do you make sure the job is done? Of course you do – a woman scorned and all of that.*

Grigor has been impulsive more often than not. He's gone through these same type of precautions before deciding to do the deed, inadvertently impressing himself with whatever dangerous act he's about to do. The "setup," so-to-speak. *Saying fuck-it is half the fun,* he thinks, that rush better than a good bungee jump.

— Fifteen seconds.

Hard to decide how he wants to go with this Isaac person. Killing. Not killing. Injuring. *Shit, who knows what's best?* Or maybe he's kidding himself. That Norm guy had it right, there's no reason to kill Isaac Stalin, anymore ... except for the pleasure and the sense of personal accomplishment.

"Well this is disturbing," The Commander's voice. Ordinarily, Grigor enjoyed these spontaneous imaginings, though sometimes the idea of The Commander was better than the reality of him. *"Where's that adventurous spirit, doctor, your entrepreneurship, your desire to test those wings of freedom?"*

— Three seconds.

— Two ...

Isaac Stalin is walking by him now, coming from the darkness into a strip of light and back into the darkness again. Grigor steps out from his shadowed corner. He's silent and quick and goes up behind Isaac and cracks his neck, laying him on the gray marble floor.

OFF ROAD PILGRIMS

SHE'S STAYING CLOSE to the wall, using the shadows, avoiding the light. *Just be a ninja,* Jessie Cole thinks. Warren had a thing for ninja movies, her ex. After coming home from biggies like *Shogun Assassin, Revenge of the Ninja* or *IZO*, etcetera, he would show her his moves.

"—Silent but deadly," Warren liked to say.

"That's you, hon." Little flirty girl.

Then he'd grab her ass with both hands and pull her to him and give her a kiss with some tongue in it – just like they do in Hollywood.

Jessie stops; mutters, "—Focus."

The emergency room is dark around the edges and bright in the center where the partitions and desks form a tight, simple maze. Two, three staff, she's not sure – maybe four. Tall windows show a clear night sky.

He's here, I know it. She had caught up with the ambulance driver. Played the frantic sister. God knows where the tears came from but they came. "Where's my poor, wounded brother, where's Grigor?" That's what she said to the driver, along with much chest heaving. The driver's eyes had followed the up and down motion of her breasts while nodded toward the double glass doors.

"—*Emergencia,*" he'd said.

Jessie Cole can see more detail now, vision adjusting to the darkness, her shoulder touching the wall. On the other side of the room, she has noticed someone, a woman, she believes, moving cautiously through the shadows. A body is sprawled on the floor fifteen or twenty feet from the woman and not moving at all.

A man?

Yes, it's a man, she thinks; then, *Who are these*

people? What's been going on here? Perhaps the man is dead, or perhaps he's sick – this *is* a hospital. People are sick. People lose consciousness. But what a patient doesn't do is hop out of bed, walk a few feet and fall on his or her face. Another thing. The woman walking toward the man hasn't called for nurse. She hasn't called for *any* help. *This woman is scared. "Let's not make the situation worse,' she's thinking.* The former Mrs. Cole isn't a hundred percent sure about that but she's sure enough. *Something in the non-funny Ha-Ha Department is going on here.*

Jessie doesn't know either of them but she bets Grigor Bolian has everything to do with the man on the marble floor.

"I sure wish you were with me, " she whispers, meaning her ex. Before she left the cab, Jessie had reloaded the double barrel Derringer. The pistol is cupped in her right hand. "This is one bad son-of-a-bitch, Warren."

"You can handle it," she imagines him saying.

"I dunno, baby."

"I do, I know."

"God, Warren, I'd fuck you right this minute. On the floor."

"You're so nasty." An amused, supportive Warren.

"This man almost killed me," Jessie whispers. "— *Mush*rooms. I still feel like shit. My body parts are worn to the nub. To the *nub.* Who tries to kill a person with mushrooms?"

"—Perverts."

"—Exactly."

Jessie is taking one silent step at a time. She keeps close to the cinder block wall, walking behind a row of beds divided by heavy white curtains attached to rollers on the ceiling. Most of the beds are empty. Her eyes are burning from the odor of disinfectant and urine.

She hates hospitals, fears them, particularly foreign hospitals.

"You have a better chance of getting sick and dying in a hospital than you do in the streets of Calcutta." That's what Warren used to tell her. Indians call the city "Kolkata" now but it's the same place – beautiful by all the YouTube videos – though a city forever shaded by its lepers history and Mother Teresa. Thanks to all the bad mouth talk of Jessie's ex, hospitals still bother her. She can feel all those tiny, tiny microbes entering her lungs.

"—Stay alert, she mutters to herself.

The man on the floor is lying in a strip of moonlight that divides the shadows. His arms and legs look oddly placed, more like a tossed doll than a person. The woman heading toward that man is going slow, *very* slow, stopping and starting as if the floor is ready to breakup and drop away. Her arms are outstretched and once in awhile her hands would sweep the darkness for clues.

"The girl's an amateur," Warren says. Jessie feels his breath on the rim of her ear. *"—No confidence, that's her problem."*

"She's no different than me, hon."

"Hey. Whose got the gun?"

That's true; you couldn't argue that.

FORGIVENESS IN THE DARK

LILI IS WALKING though the wide, alternating slats of shadow and moonlight. Less than a minute ago, she saw Isaac Stalin wander into the darkness. Now behind her, Dr. Norm whispers that he's called the police – a whisper she could've heard in Morocco. Lili glares at him and puts an index finger to her lips. When she turns back, Isaac has reappeared, lying in the silver light.

Oh shit, oh God. She starts to run to him but stops.

Her tears feel hot and fuzz her vision. She's afraid to rush to him; afraid Bolian is close. Lili feels ashamed but doesn't want to end up lying on the ground, too.

Now you die on me? She thinks. *Get up, Isaac. Moan – do SOMEthing. Complain about your knee like you've done every day 'til I wanted to scream.*

Nothing, the boy still as death itself.

How often did she and her father wish the worse on this guy? Father-daughter talks began after Raymond's oncologist diagnosed him with prostate cancer, but the doc believed her father would probably grow very old and die before the cancer would ever get the chance to take him.

His doc had said, "You got the slow movin' kind, Mr. Mack." The friendly cancer.

Raymond only heard the cancer part. That's when he started reminding Lili how

justice wasn't a given, meaning Isaac ruining her chances at a career worthy of her talent, how wrongs aren't automatically righted.

"We must pledge ourselves to justice each day,"

Raymond Mack's mantra. Like most artists he was never short on drama. "—Set our minds to it," he'd say. "You have to harden your heart, Lili, and go after that boy. Tie your loose ends tight before I die."

"We were children. Kids do crappy things."

"It *changed* your life." Cancer had turned Raymond into an old testament Eye for an Eye zealot. "Don't go thinking it didn't. And not for the better, either. Teaching high school kids band —"

"—Music."

"—Whatever." Her father's Are You Kidding Me tone.

Raymond didn't discuss an assassin. Maybe hire a guy to even the karma. Hurt Isaac, scare him, at worst break his leg, an arm — her dad stirred old resentments but left the remedy edgy and vague.

Revenge isn't Lili's way, not then, not now.

Angry feelings do more harm to the person who's angry than the person who's punished, that's her thinking, the Shit Happens Get Use To It philosophy. She preferred letting go of her anger and going on with her life.

What was it John Lennon said? *"Life is what happens while you're busy making other plans."* That's how it feels to her. Wishing away minutes on what is done and gone isn't a good use of anyone's time.

Lili doesn't want to deal with the body.

Isn't that what you're suppose to call him now – The Body, that meat against the bone? Isn't death suppose to knock the personal out of you? Everything vanishes, things that annoy, things that charm, things that grab your hand before you slip off the road.

I don't want to see you, Isaac Boy. She really doesn't want any part of it. *Who'd want to see him lying there in his white jockeys and his bandaged knee?*

She once told her father that revenge was too easily called up, too easily justified, too easily cloaked in soft and sticky pride. Lili didn't tell him about John Lennon. Her father would've rolled his eyes and looked at her like she was a mental patient.

You could drive yourself crazy.

"Hello, Lili." His voice surprises her. The man walks into the moonlight and stands beside Isaac Stalin's collapsed body. He's holding the Glock, right hand gripping the weapon, left hand under the right for balance. He says, "I'm here for you and your friend – call it my contractual obligation."

"You're him." She feel her legs and arms go weak.

"—Just a family employee."

"I-I imagined someone different," Lili says. Immediately she thinks how stupid that must sound, how anxious. Like he's a blind date described all wrong by her friends. The gun pointing at her doesn't help.

"A taller person, perhaps?" Dr. Bolian is grinning.

"I'm not sure what I imagined," Lili says. She can barely hear herself. She feels surrounded by her heartbeats. "Bigger shoulders, I dunno?" *Just shut up. This man is here to kill you. Can't you just shut up?*

"I'm glad you don't find me frightening," the doctor says. "There are too many boogeymen in the world, don't you think?"

Bolian's upper arm has been treated and wrapped but new bloodspots have seeped through to the dressing's surface.

"Let's see about your friend, shall we?" He's been looking at Isaac, shifting his attention from her to him and back again. Now he pokes at the Stalin's right knee with the toe of his tan loafer.

Isaac groans, an *uhhh* noise, his suntanned leg recoiling.

"—Hate leaving things undone," Dr. Bolian mutters to himself. He aims the Glock at Isaac's left temple.

Before Lili can plead for Bolian not to do this terrible thing, a single loud shot is fired. That shot is followed by another. And the dark room awakens. Panic brings cries and shouts from the patients, the staff, everybody.

The three nurses behind the partitions in the center of the room are yelling, *"Bajr! Bajr!"* Get down! Get down! And *"Llama a la policia!"*

Lili Mack already hears sirens on the Calle Gil de Fuentes thanks to Dr. Norm. If he'd been a normal person she'd have given him a big kiss. But he was Dr. Norm and a kiss would get him following her forever.

The first of the two bullets cuts into Bolian's left side. The second bullet misses him. Lili actually feels the air move as the second bullet buzzes by her shoulder. Right away her legs get watery again, the room tilting.

Don't you dare faint, she thinks.

Blood has appeared on Dr. Bolian's white t-shirt, the wet crimson circle growing wide, a half dollar size to a coffee saucer. Bolian abruptly turns to the sound of the gunshot and fires into the darkness.

Three shots, no pausing: *bam! bam! bam!*

A woman appears, Lili doesn't know who – the woman middle-aged, heavy in the hips, hair tightly curled. She staggers into the silvery light, dragging a navy blue carry-on behind her, the type with the pop up handle. The oddest sight. It looks as if the women is about to go out of town but has decided to stop off at `the Hospital Santos de Palencia and kill this horrible man.

Bolian fires another shot at her and she falls.

Isaac has been watching the shooting. Lili sees him staring at Bolian. Now Isaac uses both hands to help lift his left leg, his face showing pain. He takes a full breath and shoves his foot into Bolian's calf. The doctor buckles, drops to his knees, losing his grip on the pistol. The flat of Bolian's palm presses against his bullet wound. Blood is thick on the white t-shirt and between his fingers. He rolls to his side, groaning.

Who's the woman? Lili's thought here and gone. Then she thinks, *How many others? How long has this creep been taking lives?*

The Glock is on the floor in front of her, inches from her right foot. *Kill him or he'll kill Isaac; kill me, too. He'll keep killing whoever seems a good idea at the time. Just stop this guy. God, stop him.*

Lili grabs the pistol, aims at Bolian's head and starts pulling the trigger. Blood and bits of skull and brain cross the marble floor. *He can never be dead enough*, she thinks. *Never believe he can't come back. Never believe there are enough bullets or persistence to stop this son-of-a-bitch. Don't ever let a forgiving heart get in the way.* She keeps firing until the bullets are gone and what's left is the empty chamber and the hollow, sharp click of the trigger.

Epilogue

THOUGHTS ON THE
LAST VIEW – PART 2

City Morgue, Calle Vasquez
Palencia, Spain

ISAAC STALIN IS waiting for Lili on a gray and forest green wood bench in the hallway. Lili sees him as she leaves the morgue's viewing room, the metal door closing behind her. He's looking pitiful, his neck secured in a hard white plastic cast with two black Velcro straps. Bolian had given him a cervical fracture with one knowing twist. The orthopedic surgeon at Hospital Santos de Palencia fixed Isaac in a Miami J collar and told him the collar would become his best friend for the next four weeks to six months – depending.

"Hello, killer," Isaac says.

"Hey. *Not* amusing."

"C'mon. It's a little amusing."

Lili had just finished watching Dr. Padua roll the gurney with Grigor Bolian's covered body toward the individual storage units at the far side of the cinderblock wall.

She couldn't imagine being shoved into one of those things.

Now she's giving Isaac Stalin the once over. "You shouldn't be here," she says, concerned, a little scolding. "I'm surprised the doc gave you permission." She sits next to him and takes his hand, examining the white plastic neck brace. "God, you remind me of those soldiers in Star Wars"

"—Imperial Stormtroopers."

"Well look at you. Mr. Trivia."

A day ago she'd thought he was dead. Sincerely, inequitably dead. He had laid there on the moonlighted floor in Emergency, arms and legs pointing every which way, a marionette who'd lost its strings. Her grief was immediate and very strong, tears rushed to her eyes. All that emotion surprised her. Lili had almost fainted when Bolian poked him and Isaac groaned.

She had first thought about her father, Raymond. Lili didn't know if she could have stopped him from hiring Grigor Bolian, but she would have *tried* – at least that, at least a try. She would've risked losing daddy's love, if you could've call it that, stepped away from that poison. If she contemplated it for any respectable period of time, who'd want the love of someone as obsessed and dark as Raymond Mack? She'd have heard his insane threat for what it was, hiring someone to *kill* Isaac Stalin, a boy who had pushed her into a half filled swimming pool on a Christmas night, an event that brought on an ear infection and probably caused her to lose her chance at attending the Casaux in Madrid, one of the great music schools. In the end, Raymond didn't want to simply frighten the boy or wound him, this was about hiring an assassin.

Lili Mack would have made her opinions known.

"I didn't want you coming here alone," Isaac Stalin says.

"I know that now," she says, touching his cheek with her fingertips. "We've been through a lot together, you and I. Maybe you can't change history. But people can make amends. They can do the right thing. We may not have finished the official Walk of St. James, but we did our own walk. And we stayed alive, protected each other."

"God, no more hostels. I must've slept with every bed bug in Spain." Isaac rolled his eyes and grinned. Immediately he winced. "Damn, I can't ever *smile* without feeling this stupid pain. Unbelievable."

"You'll be fine." Lili didn't know what else to say. Isaac Stalin had saved her life twice – once when she was about to fall into a steep ravine and the other time had been last night. She could've never grabbed Bolian's weapon if Isaac hadn't thrown the man off balance. They'd both taken care of that hideous guy together. She says, "What I mean is, you're a very strong person. You'll get through this. We'll get through it."

"I'm glad you still want to see me." Isaac studied her face for a second or two. "You want to, right?"

"Your first impression truly shit," she says, meaning that long ago Christmas night. Partly kidding, partly not.

"If you want, you can push me in the pool."

"Let me think about it."

Lili hadn't forgotten about that poor woman, either, the one who'd died trying to take down Bolian. Dragging her navy blue carry-on behind her, as if she was between trains and thought she'd come by and help out. Jessie Cole, that's was her name. Lili had asked one of the cops about her.

Thank you, Jessie Cole, Lili thinks, the palm of her hand still pressed to Isaac Stalin's far too warm cheek, smiling at him but thinking about the dead woman. *You saved our lives, sacrificed your own to do it. I won't forget you. Believe me. I don't know if I could've done what you did. I don't know where courage like that comes from, Jessie."*

"What're you thinking?" Isaac wants to know.

"—Nothing."

"No, you're absolutely thinking. You're face gets all

scrunched up when you think."

Lili Mack is also having thoughts about how much of life is based on luck and circumstance – not just Jessie Cole's life, either. Everyone's life. Even if you don't get out of bed in the morning, you can't escape a change of luck and fortune.

That's when her memory goes to ninth grade, when she and Isaac competed for the scholarship to Casaux in Madrid. They were both competent cellists for their ages Though neither of them would become the new Pablo Casals or Jacqueline du Pre, they were good enough to induce the now and again glory fantasies of their parents.

We could easily become virtuosi to the ones who loved us and wanted us to have easy and special lives. Parents long to paste dreams onto their children.

"I'm happy," she says. "I want you to know that."

"With me, you mean?"

"—Yes. Happy with you. But I also meant, happy in my life. I've been happy in my life for years. I love my students, adore them. They are so bright, so clever. I love watching them progress. But I'm also very selfish. I love it that they love *me*, that they will remember me and our friendships and how I helped them – forever. When you think about, what else could we ever want?"

"I want you," Isaac says. He tries to smile again but just a for a moment. Then he presses Lili's hand to his cheek. "I'm selfish about you."

"Oh, you have me."

Thank you for reading.
Please review this book. Reviews help others find New Pulp Press and inspire us to keep providing these marvelous tales.

If you would like to be put on our email list to receive updates on new releases, contests, and promotions, please go to NewPulpPress.com and sign up.

ABOUT THE AUTHOR

Ron Savage has published six novels, a story collection – two more novels and another collection on the way – and over a hundred and twenty-five stories worldwide. He has both a BA and MA in psychology and a doctorate in counseling, all from the College of William and Mary. Ron has worked primarily as a therapist. He has also worked as a newspaper editor, actor and broadcaster.

www.newpulppress.com

www.ingramcontent.com/pod-product-compliance
Lightning Source LLC
Chambersburg PA
CBHW060539260626
47161CB00003B/973